RECKLESS HEARTS

HEARTS OF HIDDEN HILLS

SUSAN LOWER

TIME GLIDER BOOKS

Reckless Hearts Copyright © 2020 by Susan Lower. All Rights Reserved.

All rights reserved. No part of this book may be reproduced in any form or by any electronic or mechanical means including information storage and retrieval systems, without permission in writing from the author. The only exception is by a reviewer, who may quote short excerpts in a review.

Cover designed by Fantasia Frog Designs

This book is a work of fiction. Names, characters, places, and incidents either are products of the author's imagination or are used fictitiously. Any resemblance to actual persons, living or dead, events, or locales is entirely coincidental.

Susan Lower
Visit my website at www.SusanLower.com

Printed in the United States of America

First Printing: March 2020
Time Glider Books
ISBN: 978-1-945274-09-1

But love your enemies, do good to them, and lend to them without expecting to get anything back.

—Luke 6:35

RECKLESS HEARTS

Susan Lower

1

"Mariah, you got a call on line two, and Doc Harrison needs that suture done at bed twelve."

Mariah finished securing the sling on little Reggie Blake's arm. Poor kid had a black eye and a set of cracked ribs.

Mom stood on the other side of the bed, brushing back Reggie's cowlick. He tilted his head, trying to avoid her touch. Mariah went about her business. She felt for the kid, and she understood how young boys had the brain to do stupid things. "All right, you all. Hang tight, and we'll get those discharge papers, Mom."

Mom nodded, a few stray tears trickling down her pale face. Mariah had no doubt eight-year-old Reggie had taken at least a dozen years off his momma's life. She pointed at him. "And don't you come back now? You hear?"

Those eyes, glazed with the onset of painkillers and exhaustion, looked so solemnly at her; it nearly broke her heart.

With a rustle of the curtain and a shout from Gail, she said to Reggie. "No Superman off the roof anymore, promise?"

"Okay." Reggie glanced at his mom.

Mom nodded in agreement. Mariah squeezed Mom's arm as she headed out. "Suture in twelve!"

"I've got it. You get that phone. Sheriff Brady ain't going to stay on that line forever, girl."

Mariah's chest squeezed close. Then, lengthening her stride, she went to the nurses' station. Bending over the counter, she grabbed the phone. "Sheriff."

"Mariah. It's your momma."

"I'm on my way." She slammed down the phone, turned, and found Dr. Harrison in her way. His thick frame made it easy for him to block her. "Running off again, Mariah?"

Dr. Harrison reached behind her, and she didn't have to look to know Kim had turned to hand him a can of Coca-Cola.

Trying hard not to react to the sound of the tab cracking open as he took a swig and arched his brow at her, Mariah said, "I'm sorry. It's Momma. I've got to go."

"And I've got a patient in bed twelve waiting to have the cut between his toes sewed shut."

"I've got it," Gail walked past, holding up the suture kit.

"Thanks, Gail." Mariah side-stepped out of the way, grateful the words she had been thinking hadn't escaped her mouth. She needed this job. Needed it enough to put up with Dr. Harrison and his Coke-drinking, potato chip-grease-fingered bedside manner. She'd once heard him tell a patient not to eat the very thing he stood before the man chomping down on. It had taken everything she had not to let him hear her laugh. And she had, at the nurses' station with the other nurses, away from his ears.

She'd shake her head later. No time to think about Dr. Harrison and his contradictory ways. Mariah had to get to Momma. What could it be now?

"You'll make it up to me later," Gail called back.

Dr. Harrison narrowed his eyes at her as Mariah slipped

out from between him and the nurses' station. "You'll need someone to cover your shift."

Mariah glanced at her watch, relieved by the time. "Janet is due in less than an hour."

Dr. Harrison made a noise in his throat. Then, at the sound of his name, he turned on his heel and headed down the hall.

Taking this opportunity to slip away, Mariah practically ran from the emergency room. Her heart pounded, thinking of what could have happened this time. She grabbed her purse and jacket and was on her way.

The last thing Mariah had said to her brother was to stay home, watch Momma, and she'd call later to check on them.

Did he listen?

Of course not.

Myles had the patience of a rabbit and the mind of a mule. Of course, it would get him in trouble one day, but that day wasn't today.

Mariah prayed, hoping her brother had enough sense not to run off when he knew someone had to stay with Momma. It was bad enough that she had to take all the evening and night shifts to give Myles daytime hours to attend school.

She never bothered locking Momma's old sedan in fear the lock would catch as it had a habit of doing and not open when she tried. She could make the drive home blind if needed. With one headlight brighter than the other, she pulled out of the hospital parking lot and made the twenty-five-minute drive home.

As she turned and headed down the old dirt road leading to their farm, a sickening feeling stirred in her belly. It had been almost ten years since the accident that took her older brother Mark's life, but every time she drove over the spot, it was like walking across his grave.

As she approached the farm lane, she turned off her headlights. Lights glowed up the road in the trees.

What was Tyler Evans up to?

It had been years since anyone had been up to that old hunting cabin.

Trying to ignore the tightening of her gut, Mariah drove past the barn and parked by the old machine shed. A police SUV sat near the house. She had no more than got out of her car when the front door opened, and Momma stepped out on the porch, followed by Sheriff Brady.

Momma stood in her pearl snap housecoat and an old pair of Daddy's socks. "I called the police. I told them they were trespassing!"

"I'm sorry, Sheriff." It was all Mariah could think to say anymore.

Sheriff Brady pulled back his shoulders and rested his hands on his hips. "There's no one here, Mariah."

"I know." Mariah reached out to take Momma by the arm. "Come on, Momma."

"They're up there again. They're messing behind our barn." Momma pointed out behind the house.

"The barn is on the other side of the lane, Momma. Where's Myles?" Mariah asked.

Sheriff Brady let his shoulder sag as she stepped out of her way to take Momma back into the house.

"Didn't you see the lights? They're up there, up to no good. Something bad is going to happen. I'm telling you, they got no business up there. Your father built that cabin."

And Momma went on and on as Mariah got her in her recliner. Finally, she put the blanket over Momma's legs. She clicked on the television, and Momma went quiet, switching her attention to the late-night game show.

Mariah put the remote in her mother's hand and squeezed it. "You watch your show, Momma. Don't you worry about it? Ain't nobody up there or around the barn. It's okay."

Then Momma gazed over at Mariah, bending over the chair. "You stay away from that Evans boy, hear? It's bad enough that your brother ran off again with that boy. Nothing but trouble."

"I know, Momma." Mariah's heart squeezed. Behind her, Sheriff Brady cleared his throat. She straightened, took a deep breath, and went into the kitchen, leaving Momma to her late-night show. Mariah hoped the show would distract Momma enough to help her fall asleep. Where was Myles?

She would kick that younger brother of hers to the next county if he didn't start getting his head on straight. She dropped into a chair at the table. Her purse slid down from her shoulder to the floor.

At least she'd almost made it to the end of her shift before the call came.

"This is the third time this month, Mariah." Sheriff Brady stood, arms crossed, and used the same stern voice with her as he had when she was in high school. His brows drew together. "Now, you're gonna have to do something about your momma."

"I'm sorry Momma called and disturbed you, Sheriff."

Sheriff Brady's eyes softened. "It's not the calls that bother me, Mariah. I can't keep driving out here for false calls."

"I know. She's lonely, is all, and sometimes she forgets." Mariah hung her head. "Myles is supposed to be here. I don't know where he is." Anger burned down her throat and in her gut. At that moment, she could hear a truck coming down the lane. Leave it to Myles to pick a time like this to show up.

"I'll go drive around, probably just Tyler and some buddies drinking around the bonfire up at the cabin on a Friday night."

Mariah swallowed hard and nodded. It felt like a lifetime ago when her older brothers, Matt and Mark, used to invite their friends up there to hang out. How long had it been since she ventured on that side of their property?

Momma called out, "Sheriff, don't you be afraid to cuff those boys of mine when you see them. They know better."

"Oh, I will," Sheriff Brady called back, raising a brow at Mariah. He tilted his head toward the door, and she followed.

A truck pulled into the driveway; in the dark, it was hard to make it out, but it had dual wheels, and her brother Myles drove the old Ford F-150.

As the truck parked and the cab lit up with the door opening, Mariah froze on the porch. She blinked to let her vision adjust in the dark, her stomach curling as the light-haired man stepped away from the truck.

"Is that who I think it is?" it came as barely a whisper.

Sheriff Brady adjusted his hat and looked out across the yard to where the pole lamp sent an eerie glow across the grass.

"After your mother called us at the station, she ventured up to the cabin on her own. Tanner Evans found her walking down the road near his granddaddy's lane."

Mariah's throat tightened.

Tanner?

Her chest tightened.

Tanner Evans?

It couldn't be.

"You mean Tyler."

"No. Tanner, the younger of the two," Sheriff Brady said.

But that would mean?

Her lungs held all their air, and she squeaked out. "What's Tanner doing here?"

The world would spin shortly.

Tanner Evans?

She felt the sting deep in her chest and tried to force out air to breathe again.

"He said he had an errand to run and would stop on his way back to check on Penny."

That couldn't be right. Momma got things mixed up all the time, but the Sheriff?

Oh no. Not Tanner.

Please, Lord, he wasn't ever supposed to come back.

A wad of grief and a decade-old ache erupted from around her heart. She tilted forward a little, trying to keep her lungs from shutting off.

"You gonna be alright?" Sheriff Brady asked.

Tanner stuffed his hands in his pockets and walked up the front steps.

Now that was the billion-dollar question of the night.

She tried not to let the sheriff see the wave of nausea swelling inside her. Her heart beat faster as if to nudge her lungs to get working back to normal again.

Nothing was ever normal around here anymore. And it wouldn't ever be with Tanner Evans back.

If it was Tanner.

She gritted her teeth, looking at the devil himself. At first, she could have mistaken him for Tyler, the two brothers had similar features, but as he came closer under the porch light, there was no mistaking him.

Tanner Evans had returned.

"I take it you can handle things from here." Sheriff Brady squeezed her shoulder and went down the stairs. He gave Tanner a long look, after which both men seemed to come to a silent understanding.

She wanted to scream, to shout, for Sheriff to stay. Why was he leaving her when he knew what Tanner had done? Why wasn't he arresting him and taking him far away from here?

"I wasn't sure if you'd be home yet," Tanner said, smooth and calm as ever, while every fiber in Mariah's being held taut as she found words to respond. "As you can see, I'm here."

And a dozen different emotions she'd been holding inside her cracked open. She had nothing to say to him.

For years, she'd tried to put the memories behind her. Forget Tanner. Forgive what he'd done to her—not her, but her brother Mark.

"Your mom okay?"

"She's fine. She gets confused sometimes." Mariah said, grateful when Tanner did not come up the stairs. He stuffed his hands in his pockets and rocked back on his boot heels. Maybe Momma had been right in calling the sheriff. A man like Tanner out this late at night, running errands, had to be up to no good.

By the look of the dark shadow on his chin and his hair cropped shorter than she remembered, there wasn't much else that had changed about him.

"I figured. She wandered near the creek by our place, and I've found her a few times by the cabin. I've brought her back more than once. Usually, Myles is here."

It struck her like a paper cut, the pain sharp and quick, causing her to suck in her breath.

Tanner Evans had found Momma?
Had she been going to his farm?
Had he been here before?

"Yeah, he is. Usually."

Hearing the game show on the television inside the house and her chest getting tighter, she bit her lip against the sickening feeling that had started in her stomach.

Tanner was the reason her brother Mark was dead. So how on earth was she supposed to be okay?

He glanced at the watch on his wrist. It was almost eleven o'clock, she reckoned.

"I'd best be getting home. Milking comes early. I'll see you around."

She hugged herself, watching him walk away.

She waited until the truck pulled out of the yard, and the lights headed toward the Evans' Dairy Farm to sit on the step and bury her face in her hands.

When the cold set in her bones, Mariah returned to the house; Momma no longer slept at night. She couldn't blame Myles for falling asleep if he'd been here. So she sat and watched *The Price is Right* until she heard the truck pull into the yard well past midnight.

Mariah gritted her teeth, glancing back at Momma, and then got up to greet the tall man who stepped inside the kitchen door.

If looks could kill, she would have had Myles pinned against the wall in a flash.

The silence stretched as Mariah fought to push her anger down. She'd let it brew since Tanner left.

Myles took one look at her and muttered a curse.

"Watch your mouth; Momma's awake."

Myles peeked in the living room. "She's always awake this time of night."

"Which is why you're supposed to be here with her." Mariah glared harder at him. "Where have you been?"

"Mark, is that you?" Momma called from the living room.

Myles moved past her to the doorway and said, "No, Momma, it's Myles."

Then Momma went back to her show. Mariah stood with her hand on her hip, and her anger churned from a low-grade burn to full fury.

Myles turned with his hands up. "Don't even go there, Mariah."

"Where were you? It's past midnight! I had to leave my shift early. Do you know what that means?"

"So, you left early." Myles shrugged. "Unlike you, some of us have a life." Myles walked into the living room.

"We have a deal. You go to school during the day and stay with Momma at night while I work."

"No, Mariah. You're the one who said I would stay with Momma at night. I have a life, and it ain't stuck on this farm."

"You sound just like Matt." Mariah glanced over at Momma, her eyes drifting off to sleep as if her children weren't standing in the same room with her, yelling at each other.

"Why do you think I work nights so you can go to school during the day? Do you think I enjoy working the night shift? Or twelve-hour days sometimes? I do it for you and Momma."

"Well, nobody asked you to." Myles headed for the stairs.

"Myles?" Momma was wide awake.

"Yeah, Ma?" He said, not bothering to look back.

"It's past your bedtime. You need something?" Momma asked.

"I'm good, Momma." Myles headed up the stairs.

Mariah sighed. A hand reached out and touched her arm. "You out with that boy again tonight? It's about time you got home."

There was no sense in arguing. "I'm home, Momma. Don't you worry. I ain't going anywhere."

2

Every morning was the same old story. Tanner stretched with a cup of steaming coffee in hand, sending a curl of white mist from the lip of his travel mug as he made his way from the house to the barn. Old Matilda bawled, and the other cows moved restlessly inside the barn. A peek of the sun bled over the pastures through the trees, with golden hues and red highlights of autumn making its mark.

Tanner yawned; he could have done for at least another hour of sleep, having been up most of the night checking on the heifer about to freshen. Poor thing had been showing signs of labor for two days.

He had chased her in from the pasture late last night when he found Mrs. Lehman out on one of her wanderings. She'd gone with him when he found her out in the dark.

She chatted away, in her motherly fashion, as if nothing had ever happened between her family and his all those years ago.

His gut twisted, and not from Pap's black wake-up juice.

His brother, Tyler, leaned against the milk house with his hand stretched out. "Pap said there would be frost in the morning."

Tanner gave him the vicious brew their grandfather concocted every morning and called it coffee. "Things are bound to warm up around here, eventually."

"Is that so?" Tyler took a sip of his coffee and winced. "You know, when you got back, you said you were sticking to the farm, but then you were out pretty late last night. What's her name?"

"Dora."

"Where is she from?"

"She's one of ours. I had to chase her in from the pasture last night before she dropped her calf out in the field. You can find her and little September in the far back pen in the barn."

"Wait." Tyler held up his hand. "You named the calf September? Serious man?"

"Born in September, named in September."

Tyler shook his head. "You need a life. You're getting as bad as Pap naming those animals."

He had a life a long time ago when he'd been young and stupid. He thought long and hard about returning to Hidden Hills and couldn't think of anywhere else he'd go. He'd tried to prepare himself for all the changes, but not much had changed. Especially Mariah. After all these years, she looked as pretty as she did in high school.

Rather than dwell on what could and couldn't happen, he changed the subject. "Where did you go last night? I could have used your help to chase in that heifer."

"Out at Luke Myers' place, welding new blades on Ben's old plow. He busted two, and Luke had an older model in his equipment graveyard. I stayed until about ten, then came home to crash. Four a.m. comes early." Tyler held up his coffee.

"So, you weren't up at the old cabin?"

"On the Lehman place? I wouldn't be caught dead there." Tyler flinched; he reached up and pulled his knit cap over his head. "I didn't mean—"

Tanner waved it off. "No big. Mrs. Lehman claimed she heard someone up there. She was out last night, and I found her when I retrieved Dora."

"Ain't that like the second time you've been over there?" Tyler narrowed his gaze.

"Third."

"You think that's a good idea?"

"What did you want me to do? Leave her out wandering the woods at night?"

"I can't say I wouldn't have done the same thing. But, you see, Mariah?"

"Yeah."

Tyler sat his cup of joe on his truck hood. "You're alive, so?"

"So, Mrs. Lehman called the sheriff."

"How did that go?" Tyler asked.

"I left as soon as the sheriff showed up. I figured it was best, and I had to see Dora since you weren't around. So I stopped back to check on her and figured Myles would be there, but it was Mariah."

"Bet she was happy to see you."

From inside the milk house, Pap shouted. "Cows ain't gonna milk themselves."

"I guess that's our call to get a moooove on," Tyler chuckled at his lame joke and tipped up the coffee to his lips. Tanner shook his head and moved past him.

Mariah had seemed anything but happy to see him. Not that he could blame her. There was bad blood between them and all. Tanner tried to get her out of his head. Spent years trying not to think of her or that moment when he'd see her again. Not that it mattered much. There wouldn't ever be anything between them.

The night he wrecked Mark's Pontiac Grand AM had sealed their fate.

He breathed in the crisp air of grain and manure. He

listened to the hum of the compressor warming up, and it grounded him back to reality.

"The fence in the back forty near the Lehman's place is down again. After we get cleaned up here, I'll need you to give me a hand. Maybe you could ride up to the cabin and look around. I doubt the sheriff went up there, seeing as Mrs. Lehman gets confused sometimes."

"I wouldn't think you'd want to go back there. It's probably a bunch of teenagers having a kegger."

"Which is why someone needs to make sure no one ever gets hurt up there again."

The sound of the compressor kicking on in the milk house drowned Tyler's response. Its loud buzz called the herd as they shuffled and shoved into the waiting pen. If they didn't get the first batch of cows in the stanchions soon, Pap would curse them up a storm for all the milk going to waste. Tanner rolled the sleeves of his flannel shirt to his elbows and went to bring the cows in.

Down in the pit of the milking parlor, a wrinkled and white bushy-haired man stood scowling at them both. "Can't keep the ladies waiting for you boys; let's get a move on. We've got a day of chores ahead of us."

"Maybe he does," Tyler bumped Tanner in the arm.

Tyler whistled as he took the steps to the pit. He sat the travel mug on the top of the cement stairs and grabbed the washrag, rolling back his shoulders. "I'm in."

It took a little over two hours to milk them all, switching six cows on each side. Tanner did the washing, Pap swung the milkers, and Tyler filled the feeders and swapped the cows through the chutes. At the end of leading the last bunch of cows back out, Tyler had slipped outside to feed a few calves and disappeared.

He could hear the diesel engine rumble as Tyler left for work. Farming had never been in his older brother's blood. Instead, Tyler's talents were in his trade of welding.

Inside the milk house, the sounds of the compressor shut off, and Pap stepped out, wiping his aged hands in a rag before tucking it in the back pocket of his pants. He grunted and pointed a gnarled finger. "Long night. You catch some z's before you try working on that fence. We don't need no accidents around here."

"No, Pap. No accidents."

"Tyler." His grandfather shouted.

"He's gone already."

Pap's face scrunched up. "Don't you forget to clean out the back pens?" Then Pap shuffled his way past Tanner toward the old farmhouse. "Bacon will be ready soon."

And he knew better than to argue.

The scent of Pap's burnt bacon and fresh farm eggs in the morning had been a welcome aroma compared to the powdered eggs and processed stuff served in prison.

He might have served his time, but people wouldn't ever forget.

Either way, he'd lost his best friend that day.

He didn't think Mark's sister would ever forgive him.

He'd seen most of the Lehmans since coming home six months ago. It was hard to avoid them being in a small town like Hidden Hills.

Not feeling hungry, he headed around toward the machine shed.

"Breakfast is in the other direction," Tyler said, stepping out of the milk house.

"I heard the truck. I thought you left."

"I parked it behind the barn. I need to unload those new gates for out in the back forty. I am off today, so I thought we could get that done before Pap started harping on us."

"I'm taking the four-wheeler out to check the fence in the heifer field. I'll meet you there in a couple of hours. After that, we might as well work our way forward."

"You sure about this?" Tyler asked.

"Somebody's got to fix it. Those new gates will be the least of our worries if a cow gets loose and wanders over to the Lehman's."

"True. But we don't want Pap having a heart attack either." Tyler punched Tanner in the shoulder. "Take your cell phone with you."

Tanner patted his front pocket. "Always."

Inside the machine shed, Tanner checked the gas and pulled the four-wheeler. Then, he took the fence line and followed it around the pasture that connected his grandfather's land to the Lehman's.

Not far out, he spotted a maroon SUV going through the woods. He sat and let the four-wheeler idle, watching it leave the direction of the cabin. Pulling out his phone, Tanner snapped a quick picture.

Driving farther up the pasture and away from the vehicle, Tanner parked it near the broken fence and went to inspect the section. They had recently replaced the posts; he and Tyler had put them in shortly after his release, and they'd strung up new wire.

Tanner picked up the end of a broken strand.

It wasn't electric, but the high-tension wire strung between the posts had been cut, and Tanner slipped his phone back into his pocket. He walked through the opening in the fence and into the woods. He spotted the roofline of the cabin. Smoke curled from the chimney.

3

"What are you doing, Evans?"

Tanner allowed his phone to lower from his ear. He stared at the gray-dappled gelding and the jean-clad leg in the stirrup hanging at the animal's side. Lifting his gaze, he met Mariah's dark scowl. Her hand rested on her thigh, and the horse's reins held tight in the other.

"What's it look like I'm doing?"

"Trespassing."

"If you're thinking of calling the sheriff, you're too late. I already did." He waved the phone.

"Since when have you ever had a guilty conscience?" She glared down at him.

"More than you know." He held onto the phone. That guilty conscience she seemed to think he never had plagued him for years and gave him nightmares in the dead of night.

"What are you doing here?" he asked.

She swung off the saddle, lifting the reins down over the horse's head. "I live here, remember? Well, not here in the cabin, but this is Lehman land."

She patted the horse on the neck, walked it to a nearby tree, and wrapped the reins around a thick branch.

"You come up here often?" He walked around, kept his distance, his eyes falling on a crunched-up can, and moved over to kick it with his toe.

"No." She crossed her arms. "But it would appear someone else has."

"At least this time, when Sheriff Brady shows up, it will be on you and not on me."

"Jealous I'll get the glory?"

He didn't know why she had to rile him.

"You Evanes don't know when to mind your own business? Once Sheriff Brady gets here, Myles will be in worse trouble for having a drinking party with his buddies."

"Maybe. But I don't think it was Myles." Tanner said, trying to get a gauge on Mariah. The last thing he ever figured she would want is to cover up on her brothers doing the exact thing that had caused them all trouble long ago. It didn't sit well with him.

"And you know this because?" She huffed, moving closer to the cabin.

"I saw an SUV leave here. There are probably tracks down at the end of the trail where they came out on the road." If Sheriff Brady didn't mess them up on his way here, Tanner pinched the top of his nose. He should have gone there first to check them out and take a picture.

"Shouldn't you leave before the Sheriff gets here?" Mariah headed toward the cabin, and he followed.

The gelding stood nosing around in the leaves on the ground. At least one thing stood familiar between them. And knowing the Mariah he grew up with, she'd keep that horse all its days.

Him? Not so much.

"You trying to get rid of me?" He wasn't about to leave her out here alone, no matter how hard she tried.

"Seems to me you're the one who is shy around the law."

She stepped under the overhang of the cabin's roof. Glancing at the horse as if he'd steal it and take off.

Tanner shook his head. "I called the Sheriff. I'll stay so I can speak to him."

"It's not your business." She stood in front of the door, a deep frown forming on her mouth.

"Someone cut the wires on our fence. I think that's my business."

Her eyes, small circles of blue with flecks of gold, widened. "Are you sure a deer didn't run through it?"

"I know cut wire when I see it. No deer could have broken that wire or made a clean break like that."

"One of the cows?"

"They're all accounted for."

She placed her hand on the doorknob, and Tanner got an unsettling feeling in his chest. "Wait."

"What?"

"I think I should go in there first, just in case." He placed his hand over hers and found it cold, but the sharp sensation through his palm hadn't gone unnoticed. And by the expression on her face, she'd felt it, too.

Although, she recovered quicker than he did and shoved him out of the way. "I don't need you telling me what to do."

Tanner backed away, put his hands up, and watched with a held breath as she pushed open the door. An empty cabin greeted them, along with the faint smell of smoked weed.

Tanner forced a breath into his lungs. Embers danced across the gray ash of several burnt logs in the fireplace. Two chairs lay tipped over, and several empty bottles lay on the floor, on the old couch, and scattered across the table in the corner.

"I can't believe my brother would do this." Mariah marched around the cabin, about to swipe up an empty beer can and crush it in her hand, when Tanner blocked her. "Wait up. You don't want to touch anything until the authorities come."

"Fine." Mariah put her hand on her hip, her other hand clenched at her side.

Tanner glanced around the cabin, remembering when he'd been here last. He could hear Mark laughing, a bunch of them, as they played cards and drank a smuggled six-pack. They dared each other to do stupid things.

His chest got heavier and heavier with the memories until he had no choice but to turn away. He checked the bedroom, and while someone had slept in there, from the look of the bed, he found no danger to him or Mariah.

So, he left the cabin as quickly as possible to ease his discomfort.

He could hear Mariah inside, muttering, and something flipped over, or maybe it was the chairs being put back in place even though he'd said not to touch them.

In the distance, he heard a vehicle coming up through the woods and waited to spot Sheriff Brady's truck.

He walked over to the horse, whose head popped up, and turned to look at the on-coming vehicle. "Whoa, boy, nothing to get spooked about."

He patted the horse's head and ran his hand down the neck to smooth down the gray and white mane.

"It's good to see at least one of us can still keep looking out for her, huh, boy," Tanner said in a low voice, not wanting Mariah to hear him talking to Juniper. The gelding had to be getting up in years. "How many secrets did she tell you while I was gone?"

Juniper only looked at him.

"It's a good friend to hold them in like that." He gave the horse one last pat and turned to stand and wait for the police SUV to park.

Mariah came out from inside the cabin.

"Howdy, folks. Didn't think I'd find the two of you out here together," Sheriff Brady said, getting out of his truck.

"As I told the dispatch, someone cut my fence, and it looks like someone broke into the cabin last night."

Sheriff Brady grunted and made his way up near the cabin. "Anything stolen?"

"No," Mariah said.

"Broken?" Sheriff Brady asked.

Mariah shook her head. "They made a mess of the place, though."

"How did they get in?"

"There's a key over the doorjamb," Tanner said.

Mariah gave him the stink eye, and he shrugged. "It's not like it's a secret."

Sheriff Brady looked around. "Just a bunch of kids having a party, I'd say. I'll report it, but like I told your momma last night, Mariah, there isn't much I can do unless I catch them when they're doing it. By the looks of things, it's most likely a bunch of underage kids."

"With illegal drugs?" Tanner asked.

"No proof. All I can do is write up the break-in. I'll make a note in the report with the evidence of empty containers."

"I saw an SUV leave the property."

"Get a license number?" Sheriff Brady asked.

"No. It was a dark color. I couldn't make out the plate through the trees."

"Well, then…" he turned to Mariah. "I'd say you should find another hiding place for that key or not keep it near the cabin at all."

Mariah nodded. "Thank you, Sheriff."

"I have pictures of my fence." Tanner handed his phone to the Sheriff to show him the photos.

Sheriff Brady lifted his hat and scratched his head. "Probably the same folks here partying it up last night were messing with your fence."

"I can take you up there and show you. It's close to the cabin here," Tanner said.

"No need," Sheriff Brady said. "I've seen what I need to see. There is no chance the fence was weak and broken easily from the tension?"

"Tyler and I put those posts in before summer and strung new wire. It was cut."

"So, you knew the fence was broken?" Sheriff Brady asked.

"Pap did. He came out last evening to move the cows across the road to the other pasture. It's how I knew to get the heifer and put her in a pen before she calved."

"Know what time that was?" Sheriff Brady asked.

"After supper, before dark. Pap doesn't see well anymore, and he doesn't go out in the dark."

Sheriff Brady turned away as a voice came on his radio from his truck. Neither he nor Mariah said anything, but he could tell she had gotten agitated by all this.

Sheriff Brady returned and said, "I need to head back to town. If there is anything else you think of to help find out who was here, you let me know."

This meant the sheriff wasn't putting this on any priority list and had better things to do.

Sheriff Brady took his leave, and Mariah picked up Juniper's reins. "I'll be back later to deal with the mess after I check on Momma. Be sure you're off our land, Evans, before I get back."

"You shouldn't be coming up here alone," he said.

Mariah's frown deepened, and those mixed eyes watched him with suspicion.

"Tyler's coming up to help with the fence. Then we'll be over to help you."

"I don't need any help from an Evans."

Juniper stood as she mounted and gathered her reins. She watched him watching her, giving him a long, hard stare, and then clucked to Juniper as she turned the horse around and headed back the way she came.

Back at the fence, Tyler showed up with a jug of water and a wrapped sandwich he made in the kitchen. Tanner had almost finished fixing the fence and welcomed a chance to sit down on the warm autumn day and take a breather.

Tyler had driven up on the Polaris and sat on the back rack. "Was that the sheriff's vehicle I saw coming down through the woods earlier?"

"Yeah. I called him. Someone broke into the cabin."

"Probably didn't care," Tyler bit into his sandwich.

"Not much he can do. I described the SUV leaving as I came, and he noted it. Thinks it is some teenagers partying."

"Wouldn't be the first time."

"Maybe," Tanner pointed to the fence. "Except they cut the fence."

Tyler hopped off the Polaris and marched over to where Tanner had mended it. "We just put this in a few months ago."

"Yep."

"I figured it wasn't tight enough and came loose, but—" Tyler growled, his way of avoiding the curse at the tip of his tongue.

"I took pictures and sent them to the sheriff."

"Well, aren't you ever the cop," Tyler grinned.

"You learn from your experiences."

"You gonna put up surveillance around the fence, too?"

"Not a bad idea, but I figured I'd check up here a little more often. Pap wants to move the cows again tomorrow, and I want no more trouble."

"I'll help. I just got you home. I don't need you doing anything else stupid."

"Then I suppose we better get this fence fixed. Mariah's heading back up here to clean up the mess around the cabin, but I'd like to get some of that done, too. I don't like her up here by herself and not knowing what's going on in these woods."

"She's a grown woman. I'm sure she can take care of herself."

"That may be, but she's still as stubborn and prideful as the last time I saw her."

Tyler chuckled. "Sometimes, I couldn't help wondering if you liked that girl as much as she went mooning over you."

"It was never like that."

"Maybe not for you, but everyone in the county could see she had cow eyes for you." Tyler slid on a pair of gloves and rolled back his shoulders.

"I don't have all day to stand here and argue with you. Don't you have to get to work?" Tanner asked.

"I'm here for you, Bro." Tyler handed him a pair of wire cutters. They'd have to cut out this section and replace it to keep the tension to the next post. "Until two o'clock."

"Then let's do this thing. We still have those gates to replace."

Tanner took the wire cutters and got to work. Several times he glanced over the fence and shook his head. Mariah Lehman didn't have cow eyes for him, did she?

4

Two on. One off. Those days off didn't seem to last long, not when Mariah worried if Myles would leave and Momma would wander off again.

As soon as her shift finished and the hardware store had opened, she went inside.

"Can I help you?" She recognized him from the times she had come in before, and while his smile was friendly, his eyes sort of narrowed in that suspicious way. Maybe because, like her dad, he couldn't figure out a woman finding her way around a hardware store.

If she didn't want to go home sooner rather than later, she would have figured it out herself. "I'm looking for door alarms."

"Aisle three." He led her to the place for doorbells. "What kind are you looking for?"

Not this kind, and she took a deep breath. She wasn't at the hospital anymore, and she felt that if the store assistant came into her ward and asked for a casing, he wouldn't have got what he wanted either.

Around the corner, she spotted Tanner. "The kind that goes off when a door or window opens."

"Oh," said the man. "Why didn't you say so?"

"I thought I did." She blew a strand of hair that fell in her eyes.

Tanner turned, hearing her voice, and grinned at her. "They are over here."

"Looks like you found what you need." The man glanced at Tanner, his face drawing up in a scowl, and he moved to the next aisle, straightening up a mess of bolts spilled on the cement floor. He kept his eye on Tanner.

"Looks like great minds think alike." Tanner pulled one of the boxed alarms off the hook.

"Don't tell me you're planning on putting those on the fence to keep the cows in." She observed the selection of alarms.

"I was looking for a baby monitor." Tanner tapped the alarm package against his hand. "This is the next best thing I could think of."

She wouldn't ask. It wasn't any of her business why Tanner needed a baby monitor. From years of growing up on a farm, though, her dad had used them to keep watch on expecting horses. It wouldn't surprise her for the Evanes to do the same with their cows.

"They rarely sell baby monitors in the hardware store. You should try Kate's Kids Store on Park Street. It's off the side of her house. She's got new and used baby stuff there. She might have one."

He raised his brow, and his gaze dropped to her stomach.

Her belly tightened and curled, and she quickly explained, "Matt's wife, Jess, goes there sometimes to consign stuff and get stuff for Brooklyn. She's three."

Not that he needed to know.

She looked at the alarms again.

"These are better," Tanner handed the one in his hand, "I assume you want them for the house with your mom."

"Yeah, but nothing too techie. We don't get good reception being in the valley. I'm surprised your cell phone worked the other day."

"Booster off the side of the barn. Here use these; you'll get an alert on your phone." He traded the ones he handed her for the others he had in mind. "Good thing they didn't have these ten years ago."

She smirked, unable to help herself. She would have never gotten out of the house back then, not that she did after. Then the smile fell away, replaced with the irony of it all. Her father never left her out of sight after the last time she escaped the house. The last time she'd gone out with Mark and tagged along to be with Tanner.

It seemed innocent enough, a crush she decided had been more of an infatuation of a girl liking her older brother's friend—the one person who never seemed to give her the time of day.

She took another of the alarms, not wanting to return for more.

"I've got to get going. Myles will leave before I get home."

"I can come over in the morning and help install those."

Oh. "I think I can handle it."

"You know I'm down the road, right?"

And her brother Matt was up for it.

"I know how to use a screwdriver," she said.

"It's the door sill I'm worried about. Remember when you tried to fix the stall door after trying to lead that big Clydesdale of your dad's out when the stall door hadn't completely been unlatched?"

His fault. Not the horse. Tanner's.

She'd spent too much time ogling the man way back when. But, of course, he hadn't spent ten years working out in the orange pajama fitness center either.

He filled out that buffalo plaid shirt better than half the men in the county. Except for none of them had been convicted of manslaughter.

It sank into the pit of her belly hard and heavy. Because for a moment, she'd been able to look at him and forget. She'd seen Tanner, her brother's best friend, the one who made her stutter and her cheeks get all hot.

And then she remembered Mark wasn't here anymore.

Tanner had been the one driving, and her brother should have been the one to walk away. But it crushed them all, severed their family, and Mariah didn't figure she'd ever get past the pain of losing her brother.

Whether or not Tanner served his time, it didn't change what happened. Mariah willed the invisible shield back in place over her emotions. She learned to keep her feelings locked inside, even if it meant people didn't find her bedside manner appeasing. Mariah vowed never to let another person get close to her again. She couldn't trust him.

No, she couldn't go there again. Ever.

She took her alarms and headed toward the counter and spotted Sheriff Brady getting a new key made.

There was no way to get around seeing him with only one clerk managing the store, and she needed these alarms to help keep Momma from wandering again.

She'd make Myles help her since he seemed to think he could run out and leave Momma. A discussion she planned to have with him as soon as she saw that baby brother of hers when she got home.

Sheriff Brady looked at her, a polite smile on his face. "Mariah."

"Sheriff," she smiled while politely waiting her turn to check out. Behind her, Tanner took his time looking over the tool aisle.

"Any more trouble?" His gaze fell on the alarms in her hand.

"Nope, just taking precautions." She peered back over her shoulder and then back at the sheriff. The man who led her to the doorbells worked the machine to create the sheriff's key.

She'd lived in Hidden Hills all her life, but losing Mark distanced her from getting to know the folks in town. Marge ran the floral shop out of her bed-and-breakfast, and Marge's sister Maeve ran into the library. Mariah knew so few people in town anymore, except those coming to the small hospital beside the old folk's home. Once in a while, she treated Momma to getting her hair done over at Anne's place, and she'd grab them dinner across the street. Because of her work schedule, she hadn't seen Pastor Lawrence or stepped inside the church since that last Easter before Mark passed away.

Sheriff Brady tilted his head. The gray streaks in his hair bluffed at his age. Everyone knew the man recently celebrated his second birthday past fifty. "Listen, Mariah. I know your family and the Evanes haven't been on grand terms since—well, for a while."

"And won't ever be." Too late, she'd said that out loud.

"Don't let anyone get anything past you."

What exactly did that mean?

"I appreciate you coming out the other evening and again to the cabin." She said, trying to make amends.

"I spoke to your brother, Matt. He says there is a place waiting for your momma at Woodcrest."

Mariah rubbed her hands down her face, her mind reeling. *Tanner Evans. Momma at Woodcrest.* Suddenly, it felt like everyone and everything had turned against her.

"Luke Myers' momma has been living there for quite some time. It's right here in town. Good place," Sheriff Brady tried to assure her.

Whose side was he on?

Why did the sheriff have to go talking to her brother, anyway? Matt had never kept his feelings secret about selling their place and moving on. He bought a place a few miles away and stayed away after Mark died. They'd lost their father not long after. Matt found him in the field. The doctor said their father's heart had given out.

It felt like it all fell on her shoulders to keep it together. She went to school at night to become a nurse and cared for Myles when Momma had her bad days. Matt married and made a family of his own.

"Did he also tell you we'd have to sell the farm?" All Matt ever cared about was getting his share.

"He might have mentioned it. I hate to say it, but you were lucky Evans was out checking on one of his cows that late at night."

Mariah snorted. *Not likely.* Everyone in these parts knew if an Evans was out at night, they were up to no good.

Which was why he probably felt guilty and offered to clean up the mess he and his buddies had made at the cabin. She'd send Myles to clean it up, even though he would protest he hadn't done it.

Mariah had her hands full with Momma and chores around the house to get done before heading to work again for another three days of twelve-hour shifts.

"God knows you Lehmans have had it rough over the years, but I have to tell you if I get another call concerning Penny, I'll have to report it to social services, and they'll ensure your momma gets the care she needs."

The care she needs!? Mariah's fingers tightened around the alarms. She cared for Momma! She worked longer shifts and took overtime to keep this place going. She kept her lips sealed, afraid she'd say something to cause her trouble later. She watched Sheriff Brady pay for his key, tip his hat, and leave the store.

After she paid for her alarms and stepped outside, she found Tanner at her heels.

"Are you following me?"

"We're headed the same way."

"Isn't that your truck parked over there?" She spied the Evans' farm logo on Silas Evans' old Dodge.

"I suppose it is." Tanner cupped the back of his neck. "I heard what Sheriff Brady said to you."

Probably the entire store. It would become juicy gossip by the end of the day, with the shop owner spilling it to any of his customers.

God knew she tried the best she could. No doubt that Matt had put a few ideas in the Sheriff's mind on pushing Mariah to do what was best for their momma. Matt rarely brought Brooklyn over to see her grandmother, and Jess, Matt's wife, worked from home answering the phone and making reservations for a cruise line. Neither one ever offered to help take care of Momma. If she asked for help, Matt's solution was to put Momma in a care facility.

She couldn't let it happen. Momma lost too much in her life to be forced to give up her home. Her brothers might not want the farm, but Mariah did.

"There's nothing you can do. So please stay away from us." And she meant it, although someone needed to tell it to her teenage heart that seemed to flutter a beat whenever she saw him.

How could he still make her feel awkward after all these years and all the grief he'd caused?

"That's just it, Mariah. I want to help. I work in the afternoons, but I can come over at night and stay with your Mom until Myles gets home, so she's not alone."

Having a man who wasn't related to Mom stay with her?

Nope. Not happening.

"Thanks, but no thanks."

"Fine. Your mother knows me, she talked to me and invited me to the house the other times I've been there. I'm here if you need me. I want to help. Mrs. Lehman was like a second mother to me after moving to the farm with Pap."

She remembered the first day he'd come over, him and that egghead brother of his. They'd played baseball in the backyard, and she'd sat up by the chicken coop making mud pies because she was eight years old. Matt and Tyler were fourteen, taking four-wheelers through the woods and chasing cows on horseback. Tanner had been twelve, with Mark a few months younger. Then Momma and Dad had waited seven years to have Myles. He cried every time Momma put him in that old beat-up playpen Dorothy Adams had given her.

So many lives had changed.

What would Mark have done in her shoes?

Tanner had been his best friend.

How could she trust him?

She trusted him once. Trusted him to take her brother home. Trusted him to come back.

Then trust me.

Reluctantly, Mariah said, "It's not like I have your number."

Tanner pulled out his phone. "Give me yours, and I'll text you."

Worst idea ever.

Trust me.

"I don't want you calling me."

"I won't call you unless you call me first, deal?" He held out his phone, waiting for her number.

"And no text messages."

"None unless you text me first."

Right.

They exchanged numbers, and she decided she would change it if he called her and broke their deal.

No way would she call him first.

5

Tanner wouldn't admit that he wanted an excuse to end up on Mariah's doorstep again. Before Mrs. Lehman strayed over on their property, he stood at the end of the lane with a to-do list of all the things he could do to help around the place. "It'll take more than chores to earn their forgiveness," Tyler had said.

No matter what he did, the Lehmans, especially Mariah, would see it as an insult.

He convinced himself it was better to move on, stick to his grandfather's farm and keep his head out of trouble. But everywhere he went, everywhere he looked, made him think about Mariah, Mark, and the rest of the family. He missed them as much as he ached to talk to Mark. Would his best friend have understood his feeling then? The ones he had now?

Mariah made it clear. She didn't need him.

She never did. Mariah had always been stubborn. That was the part that had always made him watch out for her. She was his best friend's sister. No matter how often he tried to think of her that way, it wouldn't ever happen. Kissing her that night had been the best and worst night of his life. He shouldn't have done that. And they all paid the price for his mistake.

Pap regarded him. "You get that back shed cleaned out?"

"Done."

"And the water pump on the Deutz?"

He knew what his grandfather was trying to do. "Fixed."

Pap lifted the bill of his hat and scratched his head. At seventy-eight, the older man maintained a full head of hair. With raising two grandsons after the death of their father, Pap claimed he didn't know how he hadn't lost a single one on his head. But they'd gone white.

"I'm sure I can think of something else to tend to, but you're not a young'n anymore, and I can see you've got your mindset ongoing over to the Lehman place."

"I'm headed to recheck the fence."

"No need to hide your motives from me. I figured it was only a matter of time before you'd catch sight of that Lehman girl and be right back where you started. But, of course, I hoped it would have taken longer."

"It's not like that. Someone's causing trouble up at the cabin. I just wanted to make sure Mariah and her mother are safe." Tanner hated to think of something happening to Mrs. Lehman out wandering and coming across trespassers up to no good on their land. But, he learned enough in prison to know that a locked gate and a bunch of no-trespassing signs wouldn't deter anyone from getting to the cabin.

"The last thing you need is trouble. What'd I tell you? If things happen, you'll be the first they blame. It's how folks are."

"I haven't missed a Sunday sermon since coming home."

"We're all sinners, son. Just because you go to church doesn't mean you can't do anything wrong." Tanner got what his Pap said.

He had a long way to go before the people of Hidden Hills accepted him back in their good graces again. There were the ones who pitied him. Poor kid got mixed up as a teenager and screwed up his life.

They weren't far from the truth. But that didn't mean Tanner wanted their pity, advice, or judgments.

"I won't be long," he said.

"Be back before milking. Tyler's over at Luke Myers again, so he might be late." Pap walked away, waving for Tanner to go.

It made Tanner wonder how the two of them got anything done without him around to take up the slack.

Tanner got on the four-wheeler and headed down the lane.

He owed it to Mark to ensure Mariah and her mother were okay.

He rode around the fence inside the pasture to ensure no more breakages occurred. The heifers grazed in the far corner, furthest from the woods.

He cut the engine and walked the distance between the fence and the woods. Near the back of the hunting cabin, Tanner heard voices.

As he neared the cabin, he spotted the four-wheelers lined up at the back. A man sat on one vehicle, and Tanner went to approach when he spotted someone walking up through the trees to his left.

Mariah. His chest burned with the sight of her. She wore an old pair of ripped jeans and a University of Louisville hoodie. Strands of her dark hair peeked out around the hood as she hiked up through the leaves and broken limbs.

He heard someone shout, and the guy on the four-wheeler got up and went inside the cabin, the butt end of a gun sticking out from the back of the guy's pants.

Mariah muttered something under her breath. A bucket in her hand and, when he popped up in front of her, Mariah's mouth dropped open, about to scream, and he covered it seconds too late. Her eyes widened.

Tanner pulled her down a slope and behind a tree. Mariah struggled against him. "Stop," he hissed.

Against the tree, she shoved him away. "What are you doing?"

"There are men in there." He pointed back up the hill, taking care to keep his voice low.

"Men? In the cabin?" Her face turned red, and she dropped her bucket about to march up to the cabin.

Tanner grabbed her. "Keep your voice down. You can't go marching up there."

"Oh yes, I can."

"And what do you think you're going to do?" He countered.

She yanked away from him. "I'm going up there and telling them to get off my land. They're trespassing. Just. Like. You."

"Well, you can't." He stuck out his arms, keeping her trapped against a large oak. "They've got guns." He lowered his voice again, peering around the tree. He could hear the blood pumping to his heart with the rush of adrenaline it brought.

"Guns?" She looked at him incredulously.

The front door of the cabin opened, and a man with spiked hair and a tattoo on his neck peered out. "I'm telling you, I heard something."

A hand reached over, yanked him back by the shoulder and stuck his face through the doorway. His shaggy bearded face looked around. "Probably a bird, moron." The man withdrew and smacked the other one.

From inside, another guy said something incoherent, and the door closed.

Tanner leaned in and pushed Mariah to keep her hidden behind the tree and the foliage. He shielded her and stayed out of view. His eyes narrowed. A tall skinny teen disappeared out of sight as the door closed.

He headed around the cabin and saw the last of them making their way around. He hurried to turn back, then Mariah was in front of him.

"Should have known you wouldn't have stayed." Then the sound of a four-wheeler turning and returning had them both freezing in place. On the opposite side of the cabin, it sat, the engine humming as the vehicle stopped.

Mariah moved to the corner of the cabin. The four-wheeler moved on and drove down the lane. "He's getting away."

"He can't get past the gate."

They stayed back and followed down the lane. The gate hung wide open, and the four-wheeler raced down the road.

Mariah ran down to the road and stood in the middle of it, dust eating up any visibility of the guy. "And don't come back!"

"Really?" Tanner held his hands out, knowing he shouldn't be surprised. Same old Mariah.

"They put a gate across my property! Who do they think they are?"

Tanner pressed his thumb and finger against his eyes for a minute. "Mariah. I put the gate across the path."

"You did what?"

"Gates keep people out." He went over to inspect the gate. "They cut the chain" Great. He owed Pap a new piece of chain. "I'll grab one of the log chains up in the barn. I should have figured they'd cut through it."

"No. You need to stay off my property and out of my business." Mariah put her hands on her hips.

"I can't do that." He made a promise, and looking at her with those big pleading eyes gutted him. There was no way he would let something happen to her. But, God help him; this was Mark's little sister.

And because of him, Mark wasn't here.

"You've done enough." She turned on her heel and

Tanner had a sinking feeling in his gut.

Mariah punched him, then pinched his arm.

"Stop," he whispered. "You want them to see us?"

She scowled when he looked over at her. Those heavenly eyes of hers turned dark. "You're suffocating me."

His gaze fell to her lips. He tilted his head.

He caught a drift of the Baby Soft perfume she favored.

Her hands went to his chest, and her fingers pressed against his Carhart jacket.

"Tanner," her voice came out in a rush.

There was a sound of something slamming in the cabin, and he drew back. "Sorry."

"You sure those aren't friends of y0urs? You in trouble?" She looked him in the eyes, and he supposed he should have seen that coming.

"We're both in trouble if they see us."

"How long do you expect us to hide?" She whispered, finally taking the hint they were in danger.

"Shhh…"

He gave her room, not wanting to let her leave his arms. Tilting his head, he tried to listen and avoid her soft feminine scent. They watched, huddled behind the tree. He reached for his phone, fumbled with it, and grimaced. No data connection or signal for his phone to send a message "Stay here."

"What are you doing?"

"Finding out what they're doing." He moved away, kept low as he approached the cabin, crouching and staying beneath the window.

Mariah slid down to her knees and peered around the tree.

Not long after, four-wheelers started up in the back, and they heard the men driving away.

Tanner stood and looked out the window. His hand tightened around the cell phone.

Mariah moved forward, and he motioned for her to stay.

walked up the road in the direction the four-wheeler had gone.

"If you're going back to your place, at least let me walk you there, or my four-wheeler is parked on the other side of the fence up by the cabin."

She paused, flung back her dark hair, and started up the dusty road. "I've been taking care of myself and my family for years." What she didn't say as she headed back toward the cabin was she'd done it all without him.

There was a bitterness laced in those words and a pain he couldn't begrudge her. He followed her back up to the cabin, tried not to notice how she walked like a woman these days. Not that sassy teen, he remembered, and then he looked out ahead so he wouldn't notice how her hips swayed as she took the incline up to the cabin or how her curves had stayed much the same.

He liked them back then, and he admired them now. Even though he knew it would do neither of them any good to allow, any feelings to resurface.

At the spot where he first saw her, she turned in a circle looking around. Her brows drew together.

"What's wrong?" he asked.

"My bucket and cleaning supplies are gone." She huffed and placed her hands back on her hips.

Cleaning supplies were the last thing of their worries. However, Tanner could tell by the deepening frown something else bothered her. "Are you sure this is where you left it?"

She hitched up a brow, and he figured that was the wrong thing to say.

Yep, moody Mariah had returned, and he smiled despite himself at seeing her agitated and a little alarmed.

Fighting the urge to pull her in his arms and hold her and laugh at the indignant look on her face, Tanner shoved his hands in his pockets, not wanting to push his luck.

He didn't deserve to be this close to her or have her back

in his life again. He knew that as sure as he identified one man inside the cabin, but he couldn't tell Mariah. Not until he proved his suspicion was correct.

"We can get another bucket and some supplies at my place. It's closer. Then I'll help you clean up the cabin, and we can put new locks on the door after we report this to the police."

"I'll call Sheriff Brady when I get back to the house. Touch nothing. And Tanner?"

"Yeah?"

"Get off my land." She started walking back through the woods to her place.

"Mariah."

"Go away, Tanner."

"You've got my number."

He waited for her to disappear through the trees before he followed her. He stayed just out of sight until she cleared the tree line. Across the field, a dapple-gray gelding lifted its head from grazing to greet her.

He reached for his cell phone, about to call Sheriff Brady, and listened to his Pap for once. Tanner didn't need to make any more calls to the police station or need to be any deeper involved. Sheriff Brady didn't trust him. To the law, he was just another convict out for serving his time. Pap warned him to keep his head down and not cause notice to himself. Eventually, people would accept him. That was the least of his worries. Keeping Mariah and her mother safe became his priority. He'd let Mariah make the call and pray the guy inside the cabin he saw wasn't really who he thought it was, especially for Mariah's sake.

6

Mariah didn't want to believe what her heart had been telling her. It had taken the whole walk back to the house to come to grips with it.

She'd left Juniper in the pasture this morning. There wouldn't be many more days for him to graze outside once Indian summer faded away.

All next week the weather reporter on channel five claimed their sunny October would soon become drenched in a weekend of rainstorms and sputtering showers off and on throughout the week.

It could be enough to keep those guys off her land and away from the cabin. Or it would trap them there long enough to get Sheriff Brady to show up and arrest them for trespassing, and who knows what else they were doing in her daddy's hunting cabin.

It turned her stomach sour. Deep down in the pit of things, she had a feeling about what they were doing and who they were doing it with, but she wasn't sure how to confirm it.

She stalked into the house and found Momma in the kitchen frying eggs and making toast.

"Good morning." Momma hummed just like she did on her better days.

"She's making breakfast even though I told her it's lunchtime," Myles grumbled, standing in the doorway with a backpack slung over his shoulder.

"And what were you doing while Momma's been in the kitchen?"

Myles wore a pair of faded jeans with a stain above his knee and a long sleeve thermal shirt. His hair was uncombed, and he had that shadow of a mustache over his lip.

She wondered if he'd let it grow in again or try another goatee like he did last winter during the first semester he'd gone to the community college.

Either way, his eyes appeared glassy and a little red. She moved to get closer to him, and he shied away. "I'm late. I got to get going."

He tried to move around her, but Mariah blocked him. "You should clean up first. You look like you've still got on yesterday's clothes."

He shrugged, "I ain't got time."

"It's almost twelve-thirty. I had to go up to the cabin alone because I couldn't find you. Someone was up there," she said.

Myles' expression went from hard to nonchalant. "I have a test today, and I have to study, Mariah. And now I've got to go, or I'll be late for my test."

"Where were you this morning? It wasn't here. You're supposed to be with Momma."

"Oh, Mariah." Momma said, "Let your brother get to school. He'll miss the bus."

Mariah tried not to roll her eyes. "Momma, Myles doesn't ride a bus anymore. He's in college now."

"It's almost lunchtime, Momma. Look at the clock." Myles pointed to the old clock on the wall. The second hand ticked around the variety of birds on the clock face. Twelve minutes to go before the cardinal would chirp to mark the hour.

"Myles," Mariah said lightly.

"Oh dear," Momma frowned and returned to cooking her eggs. "I'm afraid you'll have to drive your brother to school so he has time to eat."

"I'm not hungry, Momma. I've got to go." Myles headed for the door, and Mariah followed him.

"Don't you think for a minute I don't know what you're up to," she said out on the porch.

Myles' back stiffened, and he paused. "I don't know what you're talking about."

"I don't work until seven tonight. Sheriff Brady should be here and gone by then. You can stop at the hardware and grab a new lock for on the cabin doors, so when you get back, you can go up and clean up the mess they left and put new locks on the doors."

"Why'd you call the Sheriff for?" Myles' knuckles turned white, gripping the strap of his backpack.

"Umm... Someone was up at the cabin. Did you hear me?"

She crossed her arms and waited for it to sink into that thick skull all the Lehman men seemed to have.

"Probably those Evanes. They think they own this whole place. Matt said they offered to buy it if you let him sell it."

Whoa. Where did that come from?

"This is our home. Do you want to let Matt sell it out from under us? From Momma? This place is as much yours as mine as Momma's." Mark's, she thought, but didn't say aloud.

"Besides, Tanner Evans saw them up there, too. And they weren't no friends of his."

"You were up there with Evans?"

Mariah considered her brother for a long moment. Why did he care if she was up there with Evans? He was too young to remember Tanner, wasn't he?

But he knew.

They all knew after what happened to Mark to stay away from anyone with the last name of Evans.

"I was up there to clean the mess those trespassers left the last time they were at the cabin. Tanner put a gate across the lane, and I put up no trespassing signs, but those fellows seem to find a way around them. They cut the chain on the gate."

"Who cares?" Myles waved his hand. "Nobody goes up there anymore, anyway. You're just asking for trouble. Let them alone."

"We can't just let people go up there," Mariah said.

"Who knows who goes up there and does whatever. Matt said you all went up there as teens and did stuff. Leave it be. I've got to go. I'm late now!"

As if he hadn't been late before.

"Just make sure you remember to grab those new door locks and clean the place up when you get home."

"No."

"No?"

Myles wrenched open the door to his truck and tossed his backpack on the seat. "Just leave it. You don't want to mess with those guys."

Mess with those guys?

"Do you know who they are?"

"Just stay away and stay out of it."

"Sheriff Brady knows. He was just up here the other day, and I'm certain what those guys are doing in our cabin is illegal. Besides, Sheriff Brady talked to Matt, and I'm sure he figured out what they're doing. With you not keeping an eye on Momma and her wandering, he's threatening to get social services involved."

"About time," Myles said.

His words punched her.

"Do you know who is up there?"

"Yeah, I do. And they just need a place to study and hang

out like I do. Now keep your nose out of it, Mariah. I told them they could be there. It's my place, too."

She took a step back. "Geez, Myles. You'd think you'd know better after what happened to Mark."

"Mark didn't die up at that cabin." Myles crossed his arms. "I've got more important things, Mariah than to go pick up trash and change locks. You want it cleaned up. So you go on up there and take care of it, but stop calling the cops and trying to control everyone's lives."

Myles got in the truck, and she watched as he started it up and spun out of the yard.

Cold seeped into Mariah's hands and up her arms. She tried to ignore it. Then, the smoke alarm in the kitchen went off, and she rushed back inside the house.

Burnt eggs greeted her.

Today wasn't such a good day after all.

She decided not to call the sheriff, even though she'd told Tanner she would. If Myles permitted them to use the cabin, they weren't trespassing by law.

It was his place, too. She didn't understand why he hadn't come out and told her about leaving his friends to hang out at their place. He could have brought them to the house. Or did he think it would upset Momma?

She called her brother Matt, hoping he'd take her side. But instead, she got his voicemail and left a message asking him to call her when he could.

She cleaned up the mess in the kitchen. Momma got cozy in her recliner and slept away most of the afternoon. Mariah did laundry and cooked supper, leaving enough for Myles in the fridge to heat later.

Matt never called her back.

By the time she needed to leave for work, Myles hadn't returned. She'd told him seven.

Debating whether to call Tanner, she pulled out her cell

phone and stared at the screen. Mariah stuffed it back in her pocket. Her pride impeded making the call.

She checked the new alarms she put on the doors and made sure Momma had a drink and a snack by her chair for when she woke. She'd fallen asleep with the remote in her hand, and Mariah pulled the blanket up under Momma's chin before kissing her on the forehead. "I'll be back in the morning, Momma. Don't you be getting into trouble while I'm gone? Myles will be here soon."

She hoped.

And she prayed Momma would be okay while she was at work. This week, she'd taken four straights to get five days off. It made her nervous, but if she could pull it off, she wouldn't have to fight with Myles or worry about Momma for five days straight.

She made sure Juniper had been taken care of, patted the old boy on the neck, and smoothed down his mane while he munched on a new chunk of hay she put in his rack. She locked him in his stall in the barn, watching him eat for a minute.

"I'll have almost a week off soon, boy, then we'll take a long ride up through the logging roads and behind the old church. I promise."

Some promises Mariah found harder to keep than others these days. She wore her sloth print scrubs because that's how she felt, slow and unmotivated to get to work.

Of course, the ER had a room filled with people waiting on a Thursday night, and flu season hadn't even come in full swing.

"You doing alright?" Gail asked halfway through her shift.

Mariah had been itching for a break to pull out her cell phone and call to check on Momma. "Myles left in a huff today and wasn't back when I left."

Gail nodded with understanding. "It's too bad it takes men

longer to mature than us women. You want to smack them alongside the head sometimes at their stupidity."

Mariah couldn't help asking, "What did Sam do?"

Gail grinned and shook her head. She'd pleated her hair in a neat braid and tucked it off her shoulders.

It was her most flattering hairstyle, in Mariah's opinion. It added to her co-worker's sassy personality. Gail's son Sam was a year older than Mariah. He'd been a good-looking but shy guy while they were growing up. Everyone figured he'd end up with Caroline Adams, but after high school, they left for different towns. Sam returned a few years ago, bringing his infant son home to raise.

"He's worse than his father, thinking we should buy a new truck for our anniversary instead of fixing the upstairs bathroom." Then Gail sighed. "But you've got bigger problems than I do." She glanced down the hall to see Dr. Harrison's spot and came walking toward them.

"You want to duck in three, and I'll take care of twelve?"

"No." Mariah took a deep breath. "I'm sure he'll find me eventually and say what's on his mind."

She'd been lucky and worked with the other emergency room doctor on call the previous shifts, but Dr. Harrison held to his convictions and upheld hospital policy.

"Mariah, you're here! What a surprise."

His face sure didn't look it.

Dr. Harrison said, "If you're not running out on us anytime soon, I've got a live wire in eight I'd like you to handle."

Mariah put on an extra sweet smile for him. "Sure thing, doctor."

Ignoring his remark about her leaving shift, Mariah figured she had a week's worth of his sarcasm coming.

"I'll go with you," Gail offered.

"Have someone sent down from the lab for blood and urine," Dr. Harrison told Gail. "Mariah can do the intake information. Or will that take too long, and you have to leave early?"

Mariah sucked in a breath. *Do not let any unwholesome talk come out of your mouth.*

How often had her mother made her write and repeat that verse from Ephesians with her brothers when she was younger?

"I think I can handle it. Thank you, Dr. Harrison," Mariah said in her sweetest voice.

He followed her down the hall, and Gail gave her a sympathetic look. As she went to go into the room, he stopped her. "We're short-staffed again. Stacy called off for this morning's shift already. You'll have to stay until a replacement comes."

Mariah opened her mouth to speak, then promptly shut it. Would Myles be willing to miss a class? Probably not.

Who would stay and check on Momma? Matt? He had yet to return her call. She could call his wife, Jess. She wondered if Jess would take little Brooklyn out and spend some time watching Momma. Then again, it would give Matt even more reason to put Momma in Woodcrest.

She wanted to ask Dr. Harrison why he was doing this, but it wasn't his fault. This was part of the job, and she'd figure it out. In her mind, Mariah heard Tanner telling her to call him, offering to help.

No. Mariah couldn't do that. Not Tanner. Anyone else, but not him.

"Sure thing," she said.

"You understand if you leave early or call off one more time. It's your job, right?" Dr. Harrison said.

He'd like that. Mariah took the clipboard from him. "I've got this."

Stepping inside the room, she swallowed away the unease building inside her. She may not have this, after all.

A man in his early twenties lay in the bed. His dark hair

shined from lack of washing, and by the odor, he forgot the rest of his body.

She pulled her face shield over her nose and approached him. His brown eyes were bloodshot and droopy. His skin was pale with a grayish hint.

She pulled on a pair of blue gloves and moved closer to his bed. "Hi there."

The man turned his head and grinned at her. "I knew it would be you if I came here."

His stark familiarity with her unsettled her. She shook it off that the man was a substance user and probably would have spoken to Gail the same way.

"What's your name?"

"Wouldn't you like to know," he said.

She pressed on, glancing down at the chart. "David Albright. What brings you in?"

"Four Wheeling accident."

She saw they'd splinted his leg, and a note on the chart said he was waiting for X-rays. Why, then, had Dr. Harrison sent her in here? "A four-wheeling accident?"

"In the woods." He struggled to sit up, and she moved to help him with the bed's controls. She glanced around the room.

"My buddy went to grab something to eat. He'll be back." The way David looked at her made her skin crawl. Those bloodshot eyes said he self-medicated for more than a hurt leg.

"What time did this happen?" She tried to tell her heart to slow. This man hadn't been one of the ones at her cabin, or had he?

"I saw you," he said.

"You probably did when they brought you in." She reached for his wrist and watched the monitor as she counted his pulse. Her heart racing way faster than his.

David put his cold hand over the top of hers and held it tight. "You're farm boy's sister. He said you worked here. Had

I known you were a looker, I'd have jimmied my ride before this."

She tried to take her hand from his grip. "You can let go of me."

"He told me to take you out. I told him that wouldn't be a problem." He tried to wink, but with those lazy drug-induced eyes, it wasn't attractive.

Mariah took her hand away. She laid down the chart at the end of the bed. Then, she walked over to ensure the curtain stayed open for anyone walking down the hall to see inside.

"Who told you?"

David leaned back and grimaced as the motion caused him pain. Good, she hoped the pain made him a bit more sober. Mariah wished no one pain.

In his case, she hoped it was broken. It would keep him down and out of trouble for a while. Enough time for the guy to get some help with his other problems.

"Do you hurt anywhere else besides your leg?"

He shifted in bed again and groaned. "My hip and my ribs." He pulled at his shirt. "You'd better check them out."

Oh, please.

She avoided his eyes. "I'm sure the doctor will be with you shortly."

She picked up the chart, and he said, "You're not leaving me, are you? I'm not finished talking to you."

"I'm Nurse Mariah. I'll be attending you while you're here in this room." It felt wrong telling him that. She didn't want this man to know her name. She didn't like that he had been to her cabin or was friends with her brother. Friend? She regretted not calling the sheriff because this wasn't the kind of friend she wanted her brother with. Myles was such a geek. These weren't his usual kind of group.

Dad once caught him smoking behind the barn and cuffed his ears, sure. Then that time, he'd said he'd stayed over at Greg's, and they'd both driven out to Louisville for a college party with Greg's brother Reeves. Matt had kept Dad from finding out, and Myles had done Matt's chores for a month.

Why couldn't Matt have called her back?

"Mariah," David said her name, testing it. "I like you, Mariah."

"I'm going to see about your X-rays, and I'll be back to check on you."

"You do that," he said. "And then you can come home with me. I've always wanted my own personal nurse." The drugs in his system talked for him.

Mariah shook her head and left him lying there. She made a note to call Crisis and see about sending this guy to detox for a while.

Gail met her at the nurse's station. "You okay? You look sick."

"He knows me, or he thinks he does."

"Girl, you better explain. Who knows you?"

Then Mariah told Gail about the guys at the cabin, Myles, and the guy lying in bed in room eight.

"Well, you don't have to worry about calling the police. Someone is already on their way down here. I'd fill them in, though, as part of the accident report, so it doesn't point to you being involved with these guys and not reporting it earlier," Gail said.

"He said his friend went to grab something to eat and would be back."

Gail made a noise in her throat, "That guy got dumped off, and the other one peeled out. If he went to grab a bite, it's not in the hospital. I don't see him coming back until the guy is ready for release."

Well, that was a relief.

Gail's usual stern look softened. "You want to switch beds? I'll take eight, and you can take the new one in ten."

"I can't. Dr. Harrison will have something else to hold against me, and I can't afford to lose my job."

"Then don't go in there without security or me, got it?"

Mariah gave her a salute as she headed to arrange for the man's X-ray and check on the other patients in her block, hoping to avoid David Albright as much as possible.

He knew her name. He knew where she lived, and his drug-induced talk made her uptight and uncomfortable to be anywhere near him. At least with a broken leg, he couldn't follow her home.

Shame, his misfortune had become her blessing.

Not that he didn't have friends. Eventually, someone would have to come for him, and Mariah didn't plan on being anywhere near to meet a said friend.

She made a note to call Matt again when she got released from her shift. He wouldn't be happy if she tried to call him in the middle of the night.

Although a nagging part of her told her to do it, anyway. She'd rather his wrath than have something terrible happen to Myles or Momma.

7

Tanner paid for the feed he ordered and slipped the bill into his back pocket. Bill Yeager leaned forward on the counter. "You pull around back, and one of the boys will load you up. Tell your grandfather those salt blocks should be in on Friday."

"Will do." He checked the board by the door, where people posted things for sale and jobs. He spotted one for the Christmas tree farm on the other side of town. Once they got the corn in, he'd have more time to take on a side job or two.

During the winter months, there wasn't as much to do around the farm in the daylight hours, but keep dry bedding for the cows and the grain bin filled.

Backed up to the loading dock, Tanner put the truck in park. As he got out, he noticed a guy leaning against the front of a truck. The guy's long sleeves were rolled up to his elbows, and the dark ink stain from a tattoo showed on the man's forearm.

A four-wheeler sat strapped on the truck bed, white and red.

While he didn't recognize the truck, he recognized the

color of the red four-wheeler. He'd seen it earlier at the hunting cabin.

"What you got?"

Tanner turned at the sound of the young man's voice. Myles Lehman stood at the end of the dock, staring down at him. His eyes weren't much different from his sister's. All the Lehmans had those intense-looking eyes.

Tanner reached into his back pocket and pulled out the slip. "A few sacks of soybean and minerals. Oh, and a bag of chicken feed."

Myles crouched down to grab the slip. As he rose, Myles peered over Tanner's truck, and Tanner could have sworn the kid turned a shade lighter.

The man leaning against the truck crossed his arms, watching them. Myles glanced at the feed slip and then at the man again.

"Friend of yours?"

"Give me a few minutes to grab this for you." Myles headed back inside the feed mill, never answering Tanner's question.

Tanner followed by hoisting himself up on the dock. "I'll give you a hand."

"You don't have to do that," Myles said, grabbing a dolly and heading farther back to the feed sacks. It smelled like an indoor soybean field with fresh-cut alfalfa.

Myles sneezed into his arm.

"Bless you," Tanner said.

"I think I'm allergic to this stuff."

It made sense. Tanner seemed to remember one of the Lehman boys had been allergic to hay. Mariah used to complain all the time about having to keep Myles away from inside the barn.

"Figured you'd be at school today or home with your mom."

"A man needs to make his own money."

Tanner heard Mariah's father say that a lot when he hung around the family.

Some things didn't change.

"It's good you're helping. I imagine it's hard going to school, working a job, and helping care for your momma."

"Mariah's the nurse, not me." Myles hefted two sacks of soybean on the dolly. "You've been hanging out with my sister a lot, haven't you?"

"She seems to have her hands full."

Myles laughed. "She wouldn't if you and she kept your noses out of other people's business."

"How's that?" he shouldn't have asked.

"Neither one of you has any business up at the cabin. What I and my friends do up there is our business."

Myles finished loading the sacks, and they went back to the truck. Tanner stood on the bed as Myles helped him load them.

Every once in a while, Myles' gaze drifted to the man standing in front of the truck.

"It's my business when my fence is damaged, and my cows could be in danger."

"They shouldn't have let you out of prison." Myles tossed the last sack of minerals on the back of the truck. "You've got a lot of nerve coming around my family after you killed my brother. If the sheriff should watch anyone, it's you."

Myles grabbed the dolly and headed back into the feed store.

Mark's kid brother had a right to feel that way. He gritted his teeth against saying anything.

Ten years. A lifetime. Neither would be long enough to put the past behind them.

Tanner should have never tried to drive that night. Sure, he'd been more sober than Mark, but both had been drinking.

It had been his fault—all of it.

He took the blame.

He paid for his crime.

Tanner lost his best friend, and he'd almost lost his life.

He thanked God he'd done one thing right.

Mariah hadn't been in that car.

Even through his mistakes, Tanner got the hunch that Myles' outburst had something more to do with the man by the truck than Tanner.

He'd seen Myles several times, and even though he knew he wasn't very popular with the Lehman family anymore, Myles had treated him civilly.

Maybe he needed to take Pap's advice and stay out of Myles' business.

Except he couldn't. Not when it involved Mariah and her safety. Tanner got in his truck and pulled around the corner of the feed mill. Taking his time, he sat waiting for the traffic to go by and to get back on the road again. In his side mirror, Tanner spotted Myles walking across the dirt parking area.

The man near the truck unfolded his arms and held out his hand as Myles approached. Myles reached into this back pocket and pulled something out. The man stuffed it in his front shirt pocket and turned to walk away as Tanner noticed no one coming down the road in the direction he wanted to go.

He lingered for a moment longer, watching the man getting in his truck. Then, not wanting to get caught spying on them, Tanner pulled out on the road and headed back to the farm.

Not long after, he spotted the truck in his rearview mirror. Was the guy following him? Tanner turned off another road and was relieved to see no one behind him the rest of the way back to the farm.

8

"Thanks, Jess, for coming over." Mariah held open the door for little Brooklyn to waltz her way right into the farmhouse's kitchen.

"I'm sorry we're late. Brooklyn's still getting the hang of potty training, and when she thinks she needs to go, we go, you know?" Mariah's sister-in-law said.

Jess had her hair pulled back in a ponytail and a diaper bag filled to the brim hanging off one shoulder while she clutched a laptop bag with her purse in the other.

"You're fine. I know Momma will be happy to see Brooklyn." Mariah held out her arms to the little girl who ran into her embrace. She picked her up and rubbed the tip of her nose with the child. "Gosh, it's been too long since I've seen you. How much you've grown!"

Jess frowned, putting her things down on the floor by the china cupboard. "Will she remember, do you think?"

Mariah held onto Brooklyn, loving the warmth of holding her niece and the smell of vanilla and cereal coming from the child's clothes. Someone liked to snack on Cheerios and most likely in the car on the way here. How could Momma ever forget she had a grandchild as sweet and adorable as Brooklyn?

Mariah sighed and put the child down. "Let's go see Grandma."

Brooklyn's bright, beaming smile, and eagerness nearly crushed Mariah's heart. "She's having a good day. She's in her cleaning mood and asked me if there are any apples up in the fields for making apple crisp for dessert tonight. It was Dad's favorite."

"It's Matt's, too." Jess moved closer to the doorway as Mariah took Brooklyn into where her mother had stood near the stairway in the living room, adjusting family photos. "Hey Momma, look who came to visit?"

At first, Momma's eyes clouded with confusion, and her lips turned down.

"Grammy." Brooklyn held out her arms; her fingers wiggled for Momma to take her.

Mariah walked a little closer, adding extra excitement to her voice. "Matt's daughter has gotten big, hasn't she? I almost didn't recognize this rascal!" Mariah tickled the little girl to make her laugh.

And while laughing, Brooklyn squirmed and said, "I'm not a rascal. I'm Brooklyn."

Then Momma's smile reached up to her eyes, and she held her arms out for the little girl. "Of course, you are, sweetie. But, my heavens child, I seem to blink, and you grew by years. As I recall it, yesterday you were born."

Momma's words held more truth than Brooklyn would ever know. Her grandma's mind always slipped and stole away the memories and the years from her from day to day.

Mariah glanced at Jess, who nodded and seemed more relaxed than when she first brought Brooklyn inside.

"Let's play!" Brooklyn ran over, and Jess anticipated what the girl wanted by pulling out two dolls from the bag.

"She discovered my old Barbies, and Kate gave her some

doll outfits when we were at the shop last week," Jess explained.

"Mariah never was one for dolls," Momma came over with Brooklyn. "I suppose that is from running around with all those brothers."

It warmed her heart to hear Momma say that. But, during these moments, she wished Myles and Matt would stick around for them to see the momma they had given up on was still living in the present.

She resisted the urge to hug the older woman. Brooklyn handed a doll to Momma and led her back into the living room.

"She seems better. Matt said she gets upset when she can't remember, and it's often. I was afraid of how she'd react with Brooklyn." Jess put her laptop bag on the kitchen table.

"She has her days. More good than bad, despite what Matt says. Momma gets upset, but she doesn't cry often. She only threw something at Matt once because she asked him to stop, and he refused. So I think he did it to agitate her on purpose."

Slowly, Jess moved away from the door. She took her laptop and placed it on the table, ensuring she had a visual of Momma and Brooklyn sitting on the floor in front of the television with dolls. "Anything I need to know?"

"She'll sit in her chair and nap here soon. She likes the television playing. The background sound is comforting to her to sleep. She forgets to turn off the stove when she cooks and sometimes forgets a few ingredients, so it depends on what she is making if you need to remind her of things."

"I don't think we'll be here that long."

Mariah glanced at the clock on the kitchen wall. "I'd better get going then. I won't be long. I'll be up at the cabin. Myles refused to clean it up, so somebody's got to do it."

"Maybe you shouldn't mess with it. I mean, no one goes up there, right? Just leave it. It can't be that bad."

Mariah hadn't wanted to download all her troubles on her sister-in-law. She moved closer, lowered her voice, and told Jess the short version of what had happened so far and while she was at it, she blurted out about the guy at the hospital and the creepy feeling he'd given her.

"Another reason you should stay away from up there. Does Matt know any of this?" Jess asked.

Mariah shook her head.

"You know I have to tell him." Jess crossed her arms. Six years Mariah's senior, Jess, gave her the identical stern big sister look she'd expect from Matt. Not that they'd ever been close because of the age gap. Concern and responsibility shone in Jess' hazel eyes.

"Go ahead. I tried calling him, and he's always busy or out of town."

"Work has him stretched, and things have been difficult in his department. They're talking about downsizing, and Matt could lose his job." Jess's brow furrowed. "He worries about you and Momma. Myles has been talking with Matt. I don't know what about, but I know Matt says that he can't keep trying to take care of our family and this one, too."

"I take care of this family. Matt has done nothing for us. He hasn't even stepped foot on this farm since Daddy died." Instantly, she went on the defensive.

Jess's frown deepened. Her gaze moved to Momma and Brooklyn. "That can't be true. He said Sheriff Brady was here, and there was trouble with Momma."

"Because Myles wasn't here when he was supposed to be here, and Sheriff Brady told Matt," Mariah bit the inside of her cheek before she said anything bad about either of her brothers. *If you have nothing nice to say, say nothing at all.* Her mother glanced over at her. Mariah heard the words; her mother didn't have to remind her.

She was wasting time here.

A small part of her tugged not to let Momma alone with

Jess. This may have been a bad idea to ask her to come over. Matt would find another excuse to sell the farm and put Momma in a home. Or Jess would see the best for Momma was right here in her own house.

"You don't have to stay. I'll take Momma up there with me if I have to," she would have if Jess hadn't offered to come over when she asked.

"The sheriff is concerned like the rest of us. Are you sure it isn't Tanner causing the trouble? It's not like he doesn't know that place and has caused this family grief before," Jess asked, her voice lowering.

Mariah had thought the same thing several times, too.

Why else would Tanner be up at the cabin monitoring the place? He said they cut his fence, and he'd put a gate across the dirt lane leading up through the woods to get to the cabin. What business was it of his unless he had something to do with all this?

"It's not Tanner." He'd pressed her close to that tree, shielded her to protect her from the creeps at the cabin. As much as she wanted to blame this on Tanner, she had no proof. And Myles had as much admitted those were his friends. She prayed for her brother to find better friends. Her family was barely holding on after losing one brother. She didn't think they would survive the loss of another.

Jess tilted her head and gave Mariah a look but said nothing.

"I'll be back shortly. It shouldn't take long."

"Be careful."

"I'll take Juniper."

Somehow having Juniper close by was supposed to make her feel better, but it didn't. Fifteen minutes after getting there, she expected Tanner to show up. It was like he had an invisible alarm to alert him when she got near. Allowing him to get close to her would only end in another disaster.

The last thing she needed was to let Tanner think they

could ever be friends. He'd been Mark's friend, and she'd been the tag-a-long. She'd trusted him with her whole heart.

And so had Mark.

He promised he would return for her. She could feel the cold seeping into her bones. The brush of the chilled wind that night on her face. She would have done anything for him to notice her. Her belly fluttered with the hope of his return that night.

And he'd never come.

Sam Brink had taken her home.

Mariah didn't need Tanner Evans coming around, even if some of her hadn't fully gotten over his absence.

He'd killed her brother.

One poor decision shouldn't mark a man for life, Mariah. But, while she heard those words deep in her heart, she had more significant problems calling for her attention.

Like Tanner wasn't a big enough issue, she had to think of Myles and these new friends of his.

She stood in the middle of the cabin, leaving the door open to air it out. Tied outside, Juniper was the only male she could rely on—even if he was a horse.

She flipped a dining chair back up onto its legs. The other sat by the fireplace, and she went to fetch it. The sounds of a four-wheeler, faint and growing louder, caused her to pause. She looked out at Juniper. He backed away from the tree where she tied him, his head up high, his eyes wide, spooked, as she was, from the intrusion.

Mariah glanced around, picked up the steel poker by the fireplace, and moved toward the doorway.

A white Polaris four-wheeler came into view and the rider.

Mariah stepped out, steel poker in hand, and waited.

Tanner Evans pulled up in front of her, his eyes narrowed. "You're late."

9

He turned off the four-wheeler. Late?

He pulled out his phone while Juniper relaxed and eased the tension of the rope tying the gelding to the tree. "Was I supposed to meet you here or something? I didn't get any messages?"

She shook her head and walked back into the cabin, calling over her shoulder. "You're predictable. I figured it was a matter of time before you showed up since I got here. And now that you're here, you can get off my land, Evans."

"And here I thought you were warming up to me." He went inside after her. "You shouldn't be up here alone. Why didn't you call me?"

"I don't have to call you." She picked up the chair by the fireplace and moved it back to the table. "You seem to have an internal GPS on when someone comes to this place."

"I admit I've been checking on the place when I check on the fence. It's easier than tracking down lost cows."

She pulled out a pair of blue gloves from inside the drawer by the sink in the kitchen area. Tanner noticed the bucket and cleaning supplies as she picked up trash and righted the cushions of the vintage mustard yellow sofa. He refused to think of the number of girls he'd kissed on that couch or the number of times he'd slept on it after arguing with his grandfather.

Something about thinking of Mariah on that couch unsettled him. Seeing her, having her this close, unraveled him in ways he refused to acknowledge. He couldn't think of her that way. She was Mark's sister. Little Mariah Lehman. All. Grown. Up.

He grabbed a trash bag and went to help her clean up the crushed and empty beverage containers scattered through the place. Near the fireplace, he frowned. Someone had built a fire recently. Ash and half-burnt logs spilled out from the hearth. Odd. They wouldn't have done that by burning unless the person had been too lazy to put the logs back in far enough. As he got closer, he hunched down. Mariah paused, looking at him oddly. "The fireplace is the least of my worries. Slobs."

"You get those new locks?"

Unless they smeared the ashes or the fire spread out of the hearth to the floor. Tyler rose and kicked his foot into the ash, the toe of his boot catching a raised stone. It moved.

"Worried you won't be able to get in?"

He ignored the barb in her voice. In her eyes, he deserved it. Mariah had never been the one to let things go. Another reason he needed to take a step back from her. In the back of his mind, the past poked at him.

I don't know why you do that.
Do what?
Make her promises you can't keep. You know she likes you.
She's your sister.
Yeah, she's my sister, and don't you forget it.

"Hard when you keep reminding me," he muttered.

"What was that?" She placed her hand on her hip and gave him one of those saucy stares he remembered when she got annoyed. He kicked at the stone again and lifted the edge with his toe.

"Didn't your dad cement over these stones after Mark and I discovered that's where he hid the key to the fridge?" They'd thought they'd find something extraordinary. Cash. A deed to the cabin. A stack of dirty magazines, but no such luck. Their curiosity had been insatiable back then.

It had gotten them into trouble too many times to count. His brother Tyler and her brother Matt usually were the ones to catch them first and keep it under wraps.

Tyler hadn't spoken to Matt in a very long time. Maybe some things broken never really mended. He got knots in his chest, the kind a man couldn't rub out of his flesh. He flipped up the rock, ash sending a plume of smoke in the air.

"Apparently not."

Tanner hunched down again and went to use his hand to clean off the ash when Mariah said, "Wait!"

He glanced up, and she peeled off one of her blue gloves. "As much as I would love to see you have to get tetanus or even a Hepatitis shot, you'd better put this on."

He took the glove to make her happy. "Hepatitis?"

"Blood. Urine. You don't know what they could have done in that fireplace." She spoke like a true nurse. He put on the glove and wiggled his fingers up in front of her to show her he'd done as she asked. He swept away the ash and lifted the rest of the stone away. Reaching the foot-by-foot square space, his hand came in contact immediately with something. Pulling it out, he sucked his breath.

Mariah's face paled. "Is that what I think it is?"

Holding up the pouch of a white substance, Tanner said, "I don't think they'd hide flour or sugar down in here."

Her jaw slackened.

"There's at least another bag, if not two, in there besides this one."

"Don't touch it!" She moved closer, grabbing his arm. "You don't want your fingerprints on them."

"Gloves?" Thankfully he'd used his gloved hand.

"We shouldn't touch it. We have to call the police."

Tanner laid the bag down by the hole and pulled out his cell.

"I'll call them." She rushed to grab her phone from her jeans pocket.

"Good. I'll take a few photos." So he snapped photos, listening as Mariah made a disgruntled sound.

"I don't have a signal up here."

Service got spotty this far into the woods on this side of the county. "Ride Juniper over in the field. There is usually some there."

Mariah made a face. "And leave you alone with all that?" she waved at the bags.

Her words stung.

"Seriously?"

Her face wasn't changing.

"Fine. We'll go together." Tanner rose.

"And what if they come back while we're gone?" She scowled at her phone.

"Then I'll go. It's not like I haven't called them recently, either." Tanner marched out of the cabin, leaving her there alone.

He jumped on his four-wheeler and took off in the field's direction. As soon as he had service, he called the police.

So much for minding his own business, he texted Tyler, the better option than calling Pap. He would be late for milking, and the old man would interrogate him worse than the cops. He would likely be late to the truck garage later, too.

You can't leave her.

Never.

∞∞∞

Mariah paced the cabin, unable to contain her nerves. She tried to stay away from the fireplace. What if there was more of that stuff hidden in the cabin?

She should finish cleaning up. It would help calm her and

help the police when they got there to see what they had found. She could look in other places while she cleaned. Her heart hammered; she ducked her head out twice to check on Juniper. He had relaxed his back leg and was dozing.

She searched the kitchen drawers to find another pair of gloves. Good thing she brought an extra set with the cleaning supplies. Pulling them on, she resumed her task of picking it all up. In the bedroom, she stripped the bunks and flipped the mattresses. She found a slit near the seam on one and discovered a syringe in a Zip Lock bag.

Her phone buzzed in her pocket.

Jess's name and a message popped up on her screen. *It's been an hour. Are you on your way back?*

She couldn't make a phone call but could receive a text. How had the time gone this quickly? It would take the police a while to come out here.

They'd take their time since she was pressed for it. Where was Tanner?

Then she heard the four-wheeler coming back. She bit and chewed on her lip. He must have gone far to get that cell service.

Either way, she needed to go back to the house with Momma. How?

She couldn't leave all this with Tanner.

Interestingly, he would be the one to find it. Did he know it was there? Did he think he'd impress her?

She tied up the bags of trash.

She realized, with the last knot on the bag, the mistake she made. Mariah shouldn't have cleaned up the scene of the crime.

You're an idiot, Mariah.

She texted Myles. *Are you done with your class? I need you to come home.*

Then she added, *Police are on their way.*

Anxiety rose in her. Maybe calling the police had been a

bad idea. What if Myles was involved? She would have to make sure Tanner didn't mention him.

She stared at the text. What could she say to Jess? She'd tell Matt.

"Hey. You okay?" Tanner asked, "The four-wheeler got stuck over in the top corner. It's swampy there."

She glanced at the mud splattered up his jeans and shouldn't have done that. Those long legs and muscular thighs of his weren't her business to admire. Besides, she wouldn't touch Tanner with a ten-foot pole after what he did to her brother.

And thinking of brothers, she needed to pull it together.

"I need to get back to Momma. Jess has an appointment and needs to leave. Myles hasn't answered me." And he probably wouldn't. He hadn't spoken to her in days. His truck had been in the yard when she left for work, avoiding her since they last spoke.

"You go. I'll stay," Tanner said.

"You go. My place. My problem."

"Then I'll go down to the house and sit with your momma until you or Myles get there. I'm sure the police will have questions for me, too, since I found the stash."

She pinched the bridge of her nose. It had been a long time since she asked God for anything. He hadn't given it to her then; what made her think He would give it to her now?

Momma had always said there was no harm in asking.

I need some help.

I can't leave Momma alone.

I can't leave Tanner here alone. I can't send Tanner to Momma with Jess there because then Matt will know, and he'll find a way to sell this farm and put Momma in a nursing home.

"Mariah," Tanner's voice drew her attention back to him.

Her throat burned, and her chest grew tight. She blinked, welling up the tears that threatened to spill. But she refused to cry in front of Tanner Evans.

"Tell me what you need me to do."

A bitter laugh escaped her. She kept it bottled for so long that it slipped past her. Mariah needed Tanner to leave and never come back. She needed time to turn around to keep him from driving without her. For killing her brother and destroying her family. And crushing her heart right down to her soul.

For these are the plans I have for you.

Her vision blurred, and the tears streamed down her cheeks. Tanner moved closer. "Talk to me."

She shook her head. Her chest was too tight, her heart too heavy. She tried to speak and choked on a sob.

They are plans for good and not for disaster, to give you a future and hope.

Hope in what? She dashed the tears away. "I need to text Jess. If I tell her what we found, then she'll tell Matt. If I send you to stay with Momma, then Matt will know that, too."

"Okay." Tanner watched her. His eyes darkened with concern. His face was etched with pain that she wondered if he hurt himself getting out of the swamp.

"Either way, Matt will find a way to admit Momma to Woodcrest and sell the farm. It's all he's wanted to do since Dad died."

"Your Mom having round-the-clock care might be a good thing," Tanner said.

"Momma's home is a good thing. She can't go to a strange place. It would unsettle her. She needs to be here. This is her home!"

She realized she was shouting at him. Juniper's head bobbed, coming awake from his doze. He glanced over at them, and she tried to rein back her out-of-control emotions.

"It'll be okay, Mariah." Before she could protest, Tanner drew her into his arms. She breathed in his grainy and citrus smell. For a second, she relaxed, allowing his hand to rub her back and believe for a moment everything was right between them.

"You're right. I can't imagine your mom going to a strange place, but you can't keep doing this alone."

She pulled back, regretting the loss of warmth from being close to him. Reminding herself Tanner wasn't her friend.

"Let me help. Go to your Mom. I'll talk to the police. They can come to the house to speak to you. This way, you can tell Jess what you want." Then he looked her in the eye, "Which I hope is the truth."

There Tanner went again with a conscience. A decade in prison had changed him. It didn't mean she trusted him.

Give him a chance. Hope for the future.

She texted Jess, on *my way.*

"Touch nothing," she said. "You're not the only one who took pictures. There is a dirty syringe on the table. I found it inside a mattress."

"You tore up a mattress?"

"There was a hole," she said.

"I'm sure the police will do a thorough search. Good thing we didn't finish cleaning up. They might find prints to tie the guys who hid their stash here."

Her gaze fell to the trash bags tied up by the doorway. So much for worrying about Tanner tampering with the police's investigation, Mariah thought, when she was the one who bagged it all up.

10

"Don't you go running off before those feed sacks are taken care of," Pap said after they'd washed up for supper.

"I'll do that right now," Tanner headed out the door to the truck. It took longer to stick around at the cabin with Mariah and then answer the questions of the police officers that showed up. Hidden Hills wasn't a large town. They had a sheriff and two other officers, but when drugs were involved, they'd called in the state boys to hand over the evidence.

"I need you to help weld a wagon chaste over at the garage. I told Pete Fisher I'd have it done by Friday," Tyler followed him to the barn. He had backed the truck up to the sliding doors and left it parked.

Mariah seemed to think he had a GPS for when she went to the cabin. That wasn't a bad idea. He got that video monitor for the barn, and he was pretty sure Kate had a second one over at her second-hand shop. He could rig it to a solar-powered battery pack, but where?

"You look like you're thinking heavy there," Tyler fell into step beside him. He walked along to the truck, and Tanner put down the tailgate.

"Maybe I am," he hopped up on the back of the truck bed.

"Not about the Lehman girl, are you? Tanner, you've got an internal compass for trouble."

Tanner grabbed the first sack of minerals. "That's what Mariah said. She called it a GPS for knowing the right time to be in the same place as her."

"You up at that cabin with her? I wouldn't think she'd let you anywhere near her. Lucky you're alive." Tyler grunted, taking the sack over his shoulder and walking it into the barn to toss it down by the old grinder mixer.

"I'm just trying to watch out for her. Something her brothers don't seem to do." Something he told Mark he would do—as a brother. Not that he hadn't noticed her back then as he did now. Just seeing her beautiful face was worth the extra hassle. A man couldn't go to jail for admiring a beautiful woman or believe she might come to accept him as a friend again.

"Matt Lehman finds out you're coming around. He'll knock you into the next county and wring my neck for letting you cross the line."

Tanner hefted another sack and landed it on his brother's shoulder. "I haven't heard you mention Matt in a while."

"We don't talk anymore." Tyler turned his back and headed back to dump his burden.

"I figured as much." Not wanting to cause his brother grief, he hadn't spoken of it. He hadn't thought about what might happen when he and Mark left the party that night. What could happen while speeding down old back roads and being out in the woods at night? No one would have thought things would have gotten out of control.

He might not have been thinking then, but he had many years to dwell on it and accept responsibility for his actions.

"If you do this chassis right, I might convince Pete to put

in a good word for you with the fabrication place out by the lake."

Tanner tugged on another bag, which wedged between two others that had shifted in transport. He wiggled it back and forth until he noticed something drop between them.

"Tired already?" Tyler's teasing jab went ignored. He jumped up on the back of the truck and helped free a sack. "You need to get in shape."

Tanner gave him an elbow to the ribs, and Tyler put his arm down to protect himself. He grabbed the sack and yanked. "What is that?"

Tyler dropped the sack and reached between them, pulling out a small clear bag. His eyes darted between the pills inside and Tanner's. "Seriously?"

They weren't his. "What?"

"You stashed drugs in the back of the truck? I know they do some stuff in prison, but this?"

Tanner shook his head. "Those aren't mine."

"They're not mine," Tyler bunched them up. "I thought you just got back from talking to the cops. Being all on the up and up. And here you are with these? Did you steal them from Mrs. Lehman?"

"Of course not!" Tanner couldn't believe his brother would accuse him. He'd made a mistake when he was younger that cost the life of a friend—his best friend. He hadn't been a thief, and he wasn't a drug abuser.

"These don't look like Pap's."

"I don't know whose they are."

Tyler's face said he didn't believe Tanner.

"I swept the truck clean before I went to get the feed order." He ran his hand through his hair. "Maybe they got dropped by accident."

"In the back of your truck?" Tyler bunched up the bag in his fist. "I know coming back here was hard. I get it, but you don't need this crap. These won't fix the pain."

"I'm telling you they're not mine." Tanner's voice grew more profound. "They could have come from the feed mill. Maybe one of the workers. They could have dropped it with the feed or when it was loaded. You should call and tell them you found it in case someone needs it and is looking for it."

Tyler eyed him a moment. "These aren't yours?"

"Nope. Take them. Call the feed mill. They could be Bill Yeager's, and doesn't he have a bad heart?"

"Yeah. Okay." Tyler stuffed the bag of pills in his pocket. "I'll call when we get done and leave a message for Bill."

Satisfied, Tyler helped him finish unloading the rest of the feed sacks.

"Who helped you load this, anyway?" Tyler asked.

"Myles Lehman."

Deciding it best his brother knew he wouldn't ever hide anything from him, Tanner told him about the guys on four-wheelers up at the Lehman hunting cabin, the stash of drugs he found in the fireplace, and the local law enforcement called in the state police.

Tyler listened. Tanner had his brother's full attention. He told him about the guy at the feed mill, and Myles' encounter, all the while leaving his conflicting feelings about Mariah out of it. He pulled out his cell phone and showed him the pictures.

"I don't want Pap to worry, so I'd prefer we say nothing to him."

Tyler crossed his arms and lowered his chin. "I think that's a good idea. And from now on, I think you need to stay clear of that place."

He planned on it. God knew the reason for all this. Why else would he have been the one to find Mrs. Lehman out wandering? He spent a lot of nights in prison, lying in a narrow cot and having conversations with the man upstairs in his head. A few with Mark. Mostly apologies. *There is a higher purpose in all of this. Trust Him.*

It had been one thing Mrs. Lehman had written him in the letters she sent him faithfully in the early years of his imprisonment.

"I can't." Tanner looked at his brother. "Someone has to look out for them."

"I believe that's God's job. Yours is getting that wagon frame fixed. It doesn't take getting involved with a Lehman to do that."

No, he didn't suppose it did.

Mariah kept telling him to go away.

He should listen, stay away, and decide it best he did. He wouldn't go there. Not unless Mariah asked him.

After Jess had brought the baby, Momma had mentioned no one else coming to the house in a few days. While she had settled in Daddy's old chair watching another one of those daytime talk shows Mariah despised, Mariah slipped out to the barn to check on Juniper.

Even a few minutes out of the house and away from the hospital brought a sense of peace to her troubled soul.

People came in looking for help for all kinds of ailments and injuries. Yesterday, an older man had fallen off the roof of the local bank, and she helped stabilize him enough for him to be transported to Louisville to a bigger hospital.

This morning as she ended her shift, an elderly couple sat in room six, holding hands. The eyes of the older gentleman fixated on his wife, memorizing her, photographing her in his heart for all time. Beside them, an adult child read from the Bible. It soothed the couple and those who could hear the passages read.

It made Mariah think of the last time she'd opened her Bible in the busyness of trying to keep up with everything.

Last Sunday had been the first in a month she'd gone and made it to sit in the last pew by Ann Fisher and her boys.

She took a bucket from the porch and filled it in the kitchen before heading to the barn. One of these days, she'd have to suck it up and ask someone to help fix the faucet in the barn since Myles had no interest in doing anything around the farm.

Halfway across the yard, Mariah dropped the bucket of water.

It sloshed over her pant leg.

Her heart caught in her throat.

Someone had graffitied a nasty warning on the side of the barn.

She went to check on Juniper.

"Juniper?"

She found his stall empty. "Juniper?"

She heard the whinny and went to the back door leading to the pasture, finding it open. The dapple-gray gelding stood outside with the breeze, lifting parts of his dark mane to float in the wind.

At hearing his name, he started back toward the barn. Joy released the tightness of panic.

How long had he been out there?

No matter. Mariah rushed to him and checked him over for any signs of harm. Finding none, she wrapped her arms around his thick neck before deciding best to feed him outside this morning. A brush of frost tipped the grass from last night's lower temperatures. Otherwise, Juniper went back to his spot where he'd been grazing. She shut the door to keep him out.

Juniper's stall door was tossed off the tracks, and a few hundred pounds of horse feed ruined on the floor, mixed with saddle soap and diesel fuel spilled from a spare can he kept in the tool shed.

She pulled out her phone, scrolled down through it, and

hit the call button. When she heard a voice answer, she blurted, "Someone vandalized the barn."

"I'm on my way,"

No. Wait.

Tanner?

She called Tanner?

Mariah looked at her phone.

Sure enough, she called him first. His name had been listed under 'sheriff' for the police station, and she'd accidentally touched his name.

Stupid fat fingers.

She touched the correct name, the number popping up, and called the police this time. The dispatcher said, "I'll send someone out. Touch nothing until one of ours gets there."

She heard the truck and the slam of the door. She met Tanner at the entrance.

"You okay?"

"It must have happened last night while I was on shift."

"Where's Myles?"

"Early morning class. Myles usually leaves by seven-thirty on Thursdays. I didn't get home until almost nine. I couldn't leave my patient until they found another staff member to sit with her. She was a high risk."

One too many she'd faced this past week, trying not to let her exhaustion show. Dr. Harrison had made a point after the first one to see she got all the high-risk and high-maintenance patients.

Tanner ran his hand through his hair. He had on a pair of rubber barn boots and overhauls with a washrag hanging out of his side pocket. "You were still milking?"

"Late start. The compressor wasn't working."

"Something didn't happen to it, did it?"

Those seconds of panic built again until he said, "Just old."

"Well, I'm sorry I accidentally called you when I tried calling the police. You can get back to your milking now."

"Tyler can finish up. After that, it's his turn to wash down the parlor." He referred to the room where the cows walked in to get milked. It had a pit in the middle, and six cows could walk in line to eat and get milked on each side.

She had gone over many times to help feed the calves as an excuse so she could spend time with him. Her father used to tell her he could give her more chores and that she didn't need to go to the Evans place to do theirs. But her father raised horses and a few beef cattle for the freezer. Sometimes, Mr. Evans would let her bring milk home for Momma to make butter in her old electric churn.

"Anything missing?"

Time to pull it together, Mariah, and get your head out of the past.

"Not missing. Destroyed. They left a warning on the side of the barn." She pointed. "Touch nothing. I have to check on Momma. I don't want her seeing this or getting upset when another police cruiser pulls in the yard."

"That answers my next question." He walked over to view the spray-painted words.

Far from pretty, the vulgar warning made her legs a little weak.

"I should have seen this coming. No one will walk away from losing that kind of stash like we found in the cabin."

Mariah frowned. Hugging herself, her mind recalled the man in the hospital, David, something. And she'd been up to the cabin. Her skin prickled with tiny bumps under her jacket. "Sheriff Brady has it."

"They will not care," Tanner scowled. "You and your mother shouldn't be alone. Not until the police catch these guys."

She put her hands on her hips and gave him a look she used on her brothers when they tried to coerce her into staying behind or trying to get rid of her for their devious schemes. She should have known better, though, for it never seemed to affect Tanner.

He could be twice as stubborn. Or at least he had been the night Mark died. She wrapped that sorrow away and kept it for another day.

And what he said made sense. It scared her. What would happen if she wasn't here? What if Myles didn't come home on time? Would they hurt Momma?

The threat on the barn said they would.

Tanner stepped closer. His voice lowered a rough edge that rippled through her defiance. "I mean it, Mariah. You and your mom are here practically alone all the time. Use your head. Stay safe."

She bristled at his words. "I'm not stupid. I know how to take care of myself and watch out for Momma."

Tanner frowned, those eyes of his tugging to pull her into whatever pit he trapped her into all those years ago. It was hard to look away. Not that he'd ever seen her the way she'd hoped he would.

"I've met guys like this. You don't want to mess with them."

"In prison, you mean?"

"Yeah, and I've seen one of them. I recognized the four-wheeler from the cabin. He had it on the back of a truck parked behind the feed mill."

She crossed her arms. "Because people who do bad things hang out behind the feed mill."

"He was waiting for Myles, and I saw them exchange something."

"Myles doesn't work at the feed mill anymore. He goes to college full time."

"That's why he loaded my truck with Pap's feed order." Tanner grabbed her by both arms. "Listen, it's not my business what Myles does, but don't expect me to stand back while you put yourself in danger."

11

Mariah paled, her hands at her sides, clenching and releasing as if she would punch him. Her dark hair pulled back, and the scent of hospital mixed with cooked eggs couldn't have been a further deterrent. Then he looked into those eyes, wide, beautiful, and proud. His or hers? He saw his own emotions reflecting in those blue orbs. Fear, admiration, and desperation gripped him at the knees and almost took him down.

He held her gaze briefly before it dropped to her quivering lip. More of her fighting her pride or coming up with a clever retort. He wouldn't let her get the words out.

He couldn't take it. An urge, an impulse to close the rift between them, surged through him as quickly as the desire to act hit him.

Tanner kissed her. Not the tentative first kiss he always imagined they would share. Soft, sweet, and probing. No, this kiss he'd wanted since he got in the car with her brother that night, torn between letting Mark drive away to do something even more stupid than driving drunk. He'd seen her laughing and flirting with Sam Brink near the bonfire.

No, he kissed her as a man possessed. He slipped his hand

up around her neck, drawing her in. She reached up, grabbed the wrinkle in his overhauls, leaning against him.

He lost himself in the sensation. Mariah's mouth was soft and willing under his.

Ignoring the voice in the back of his head, reminding him she was off-limits or that she'd hate him later, Tanner gave in to wrapping his other arm around her.

A sound came across the yard, like a screen door slapping against the doorjamb. Mariah stiffened and pulled away. Maybe she'd read his thoughts, or they could call it divine intervention, for it should never have happened.

His heart was beating wildly in his chest as he leaned back.

She lifted her gaze to meet his, her eyes glassy and intoxicated by the kiss they shared.

"Mariah?" Mrs. Lehman's voice floated across the yard.

Tanner loosened his hold on her.

Slowly, she turned her head away from him. "It's alright, Momma. I'll be there in a minute."

Maybe for her. Tanner tried to catch his breath and be cool about it. But something about Mariah's mother finding them together made him feel juvenile and guilty.

She took a long breath and let it out slowly. "I have to go check on Momma."

It wrenched his gut that she wouldn't look at him. He grabbed her hands. "Wait. Mariah."

There were things he needed to say.

"I've got to call the sheriff. This shouldn't have happened."

He wanted to blame it on a lack of oxygen or the adrenaline still surging in his veins because he couldn't explain his lack of self-discipline for using it as an excuse to kiss his best friend's sister.

Dead best friend.

"I'll call the sheriff. You head to the house before your mom finds her way out here."

She clamped her mouth shut, nodded, and walked away from him.

"Go on," he muttered, hating himself for allowing the distance to stretch between them once more.

Reaching inside his pocket, he pulled out his phone. Then, muttering, "God help me," he called the police station and explained the situation.

Careful not to disturb the mess, Tanner took pictures of the graffiti and destruction. However, he didn't dare go in the barn in case his footsteps imprinted and caused him to look more suspect than innocent.

He welcomed the drizzle of rain that greeted him as he went to his truck. He sat in the driver's seat, waiting for one of the Sheriff's men to show, and watched Mariah through the living room window. She stood, her back to him, and bent as she talked to her mother.

His phone pinged with a text from Tyler. Part of him wanted to text back and tell his brother he'd locked lips with Mariah. The other part winced, thinking of the slap upside the head his brother would give him.

Reluctant to reply at all, he stared at Tyler's question. "What are you up to?"

"What do you need?" Tanner spoke as his fingers moved to answer. Tyler only called or texted when he needed something. Why wouldn't he? Not as if they didn't both live in the same place.

For the longest time, Tyler had been angry with him. It took a few years before his brother came around to visit him or gift money to his account for him to call home. There had been little to say. What they shared came from the farm, and no news anywhere else. When he asked, the questions had gone ignored.

Ten years had been a long time away from his family. He couldn't compare it to the loss he caused both their families.

Tanner bowed his head in grief and regretted his constant companion inside the truck cab.

He pressed his hand to his chest and tried to push against the ache that never seemed to go away. A pain that grew as he sat there, gazing ahead to the window. His chest was tighter, his head clouded with the consequences of his actions.

What are you waiting for? Let's get going!

Mark's voice in his head made him jolt a little. He sucked in his breath at the memory. Seventeen-year-old Mark sat across from him. He hadn't heard the truck door slam shut, and his best friend crossed his arms. He'd been sitting there a minute too long. By the look on his face, he had grown impatient.

You keep looking at her like that, and she'll think you like her.

Tanner had made a noise in the back of his throat. Like Mariah? No. Just no. She was annoying. Tanner started the truck and heard the engine turn over and idle. Pap's chunky beef stew still searching to settle since he'd inhaled his supper to get over to the Lehman's in time to pick up Mark.

She wore those tall black rubber boots and one of her dad's old flannel shirts. Heaven forbid she get one of her own dirty doing chores. He'd seen the blouse beneath, and if they didn't get going, she'd try to tag along.

Are we going or what? Angie's waiting, man.

Angie Brothers was Mark's current fling.

Tanner took a deep breath and pushed Mark and the memory away.

Sorry man, I can't go back there again. Tanner lifted his gaze back to the living room window and the present. Where had Mariah gone?

Tapping on the window made him jump. Standing by the door, her arms crossed, Mariah glared at him.

Would she want to talk about the kiss?

She'd make it out to be a mistake. A mistake he'd happily

do over again. More gold than blue in her eyes, trickles of rain streaming down in slow, small thin lines on the window.

He rolled down the glass. "They're sending someone over. I'll stay until they get here."

"I think you should leave." She pulled up her hood in the rain.

His phone pinged, and he glanced at the text. "Meet me down at the truck garage."

"Please, just leave." The strain in her voice caused him to forget about the text and everything except her. She turned and walked back to the house in a hurry. More to escape the rain falling more steadily than before than to get away from him. Or maybe a little of both.

Leave her. She'll just slow us down.

About to tell the voice otherwise, Tanner looked over at the empty seat beside him. Mark's ghost would forever haunt him if he let it.

Slowing down was not a bad thing back then.

Tanner replied to Tyler. "On my way."

What would he have to do for Mariah to forgive him?

Mariah led her mother back inside the house. Penny Lehman's eyes filled with childlike curiosity. "Who was that in the truck? Silas, come looking for one of his boys again?"

"No, Momma. It was Tanner," she said, not that Momma would remember later.

Momma wore a pair of sweatpants and a collared shirt with daisies stitched on the sleeves.

"Looking to run off with Mark," Momma muttered.

"Mark's not here," she hated having to remind her. "He died, remember."

Momma's eyes glistened with confusion. Inside the

kitchen, she fussed, pulling out a kettle to make tea. "Your daddy's gone."

"And Mark," Mariah pulled down her hood, shivered from the icy rain, and the warmth of walking into the house sent little bumps racing up her arms.

"I know." Momma glanced over her shoulder at Mariah. For one of those fleeting moments, Mariah could see the truth in her momma's eyes. "Not all those who are lost are gone forever."

And there it was, the moment came and went with a little of Momma's random wisdom.

She was in there somewhere. Mariah stayed out of the way as her mother made tea, but she grabbed a piece of shortbread from the canister by the stove.

She glanced at the little weekly pill dispenser and frowned. "Momma, you take your medicine today?"

Momma waved her hand. "You know I can't remember those things. What's the container say?"

"It's empty, and it's only Saturday. There should be another day here?"

Mariah reached up in the cupboard and checked her mother's medicine bottles. She refilled them every Sunday. Had she forgotten everything going on? Had Myles given Momma two days in one?

No. Mariah's gut told her she wouldn't have forgotten to refill it. Myles knew Momma needed her medicine every night before bed. She filled the container, determined to move on and not dwell on the things she couldn't change.

By then, the police cruiser pulled into the yard, and her mother went to the door. "Good heavens, what trouble is there now?"

Hearing the panic in her mother's voice, Mariah put her hand on her mother's arm. "It's okay, Momma. I called them. They're here to see me."

Momma's eyes narrowed. "Mariah Doreen Lehman, you

know you're supposed to tattle to your daddy or me before calling the cops. Not everything those brothers of yours does is worthy of getting them arrested. I know you want nothing more than to be rid of those boys, but this isn't the way."

Mariah resisted the urge to roll her eyes. "This has nothing to do with my brothers."

She hoped.

"Someone vandalized the barn. So I called the cops to report it."

Momma's eyes widened, and she gripped Mariah's arms in return. "It's those hoodlums that were up at the cabin, isn't it? They came and destroyed stuff in our barn. I told the Sheriff."

"Yes, Momma. It's just some spray paint, and they tipped things over. I'll clean it up as soon as the police look at it."

Momma reached for the door as the officer stepped on the porch. The tea kettle screamed, and Momma turned away to tend it.

Mariah opened the door to greet the man in uniform. "One moment." Mariah turned the stove off, and Momma took her tea in the living room. The plate of shortbread was gone with it.

"Thank you for your patience," she said. "Someone vandalized our barn."

Sheriff Brady had sent a new officer, probably a guy stuck to his desk most of the time. He walked around inside the barn and asked questions. She spied a few of them written on the notepad in his hand.

He made notes and looked around outside before coming back into the barn out of the rain.

The sounds of it hitting the metal roof made it hard to speak. Finally, the officer had to shout a little. "Any idea who did this?"

"We've been having trouble up at my dad's old hunting

cabin. I reported it, and I believe the neighbors have had some trouble with having their fence cut." She shouldn't have brought up Tanner. She asked him to leave, never expecting him to listen.

"This isn't far from where the drugs were found?"

"That's right. It was my dad's hunting cabin up in the woods."

"Did you see anyone before this happened?"

Tanner Evans. She seemed to see him all the time these days, and he'd gotten entirely too friendly.

Shame there was no law against it.

She called him. And he'd come.

She shook her head. "No, but my horse wasn't in the barn. I didn't know if they left him out or my brother did. He's usually locked in at night with this weather."

"Where is your brother now?"

Good question. Myles was still avoiding her.

"I don't know. He doesn't tell me where he goes. He's taking classes at the local community college. He could have gone to hang out with friends or to study at the library."

Both are excellent possibilities.

It worried her about the friends he hung out with. Neither did she believe he would study at the library on a Saturday. But, of course, she wouldn't share her concerns with the police officer.

"My brother wouldn't have done this."

"But he could have left the horse out?"

"Yeah, he lives here and helps out. Sheriff Brady knows this, too."

The officer closed his notepad and slipped it into a sleeve on his belt. "Can I see the horse?"

"He's standing behind the barn under the overhang of the roof. I didn't want to put him back in until I could clean this up."

"Understood. I'll take a walk around there and check him

out. You should be able to clean it up and put your animal back inside when I'm finished."

"His name is Juniper." She got the distinct feeling the guy liked horses.

He grinned at her. "I'll take a few pictures, it'll be hard to get them outside in the rain, but it's the best I can do."

It was all she could expect him to do on a miserable day like this.

Sitting in his car to write up his report took him another twenty minutes.

She half expected half hoped, Tanner would appear back in her driveway.

She shouldn't. She tried to hate him. Hate what he did. And it tore her almost in two.

Returning to the house, Mariah's heart skidded to a stop. "Momma?"

The living room was empty, and a rerun sitcom was on the television.

12

"Pap called. Mrs. Lehman came over for tea and cookies. He wants one of us to take her back home. He got an earful about us boys causing trouble for her girl and something about vandalizing the barn."

Tanner tossed down the last rack boards from the old hay wagon. "She's confused. Something must have happened that Mariah didn't catch her leaving the house."

Surely, Mariah would have installed those alarms she purchased by now.

"It's gotten that bad?" Pete wiped the sweat off his face on the bottom hem of his stained shirt.

"Which part?" Tyler reached for a water jug, took a gulp, and grunted. "This isn't the first time Mrs. Lehman has gone for a walk, and Tanner has taken her home."

Pete's brow rose. "You know I don't like to gossip, but Anne said she'd heard Penny Lehman's dementia had worsened since Robert passed. We've been praying for her and the family in church. It must be hard for all of them."

"It doesn't seem to end," Tanner tossed his hammer back on the workbench. "I'll take Mrs. Lehman home. Mariah must be frantic. After what happened to the barn, it must have upset her mom, too."

"Something happened at the barn?" Tyler asked.

"Yeah, this morning. Graffiti and trashed the inside."

Tyler tilted his head. "And you know this because?"

"She called me. I went over." He turned away before his brother could see any other kind of guilt written on his face.

"She called you?" Pete leaned back against a wagon tire. "Didn't figure I'd ever see the day the Lehmans and the Evans were on speaking terms again."

"That makes two of us." Tyler glared at Tanner. "Tanner here has been warned to stay away, but for some reason, he seems to think he needs to get involved in their business. You know you don't have to earn their forgiveness. You were both victims of what happened."

Pete brushed his hair back, a little thinner on top from when Tanner last remembered him.

"Some people don't see it that way. It's a shame. Not everyone can let things go at the same time. I'm sorry it's affected your ability to get work outside the farm. Tyler said no one would hire you, and you shouldn't have to prove yourself since you've already paid for what happened."

"It wasn't anyone's fault," Tyler said.

"It was mine." Tanner had years to own up to his mistake. "I was the one driving. I could have said no, but I knew if I didn't drive or if I didn't go along, Mark would find a way to get in more trouble. Angie was two-timing him, and I figured I should be there when he found out."

"That's rough," Pete said. "You need to let it go and move on. Maybe when you do, others will too."

"I'd best go get Mrs. Lehman," Tanner said.

"I'll go with you. It's been a while since I've seen Mrs. Lehman. We'll take my truck and come back for the other one."

They rode in silence until they got to the farm lane. "Pete's right. You need to let go and move on. You've got a second chance. We get Mrs. Lehman home. Then it would be best to avoid them, especially with this drug business."

And leave Mariah to handle it alone.

"It'll get worse if no one stops it. What happens when it trickles to our farm? It will if we don't stop it."

"Let the police handle it."

"I am."

They pulled up by the old farmhouse. The rain continued coming down in a drizzle and splashing on the windshield. Heat burst from the dash, the warm air sending slight chills through him.

"I'm not trying to earn anyone's forgiveness, Ty."

Tanner could taste Mariah's kiss lingering on his lips. Her body had gone lax for a few seconds while he held her. Had he always loved her?

It was hard for him to say.

"Then, what are you doing?" Tyler asked.

Tanner reached for the door lever. "Trying to keep anyone else from dying."

Their grandmother never fussed with pretty things, finding joy in the simple. She loved her ducks and daisies, and her kitchen looked like a spring pond with blue walls and white-washed countertops.

Tanner had few memories of the woman who made sure he and his brother had a home, food, and a place to call their own. He had even fewer memories of the people responsible for bringing him into this world. Tyler had been older and remembered more, but their grandmother held and loved them for a short time. It had been Pap who saw them through the troubled years. And there had been many.

Tanner expected to find Mrs. Lehman in the kitchen.

Pap hobbled around the doorway.

"Where is Mrs. Lehman?" Tyler asked, reaching to swap his damp jacket for a drier one on the coat stand.

"You took too long. She's gone."

"You took her home?" Tanner asked.

"She can walk. She walked herself here, didn't she?" Tanner couldn't believe it. "In the rain? On her own?"

"The woman is demented," Tyler's eyes darkening to match Tanner's mood.

"She came and said her peace. Nothing unbalanced about that. A little rain never killed anybody."

No. It most certainly didn't.

Tanner noticed the way Pap flinched. His face was haggard, and his gait was off today. The cold setting in with the rain went straight to the ache of his old bones. Tanner lifted his ball cap and ran his hand through his hair.

"I'll go see if I can find her. Make sure she gets home safe."

"I'll go with you," Tyler said.

"Don't take too long. A storm is coming, and I want those cows brought in before we get any lightning."

"She's probably home by now," Tyler said.

For Mariah and Mrs. Lehman's sake, Tanner hoped. *But, please, Lord, let Mrs. Lehman be home safe and warm from this weather with Mariah.*

It occurred to him then Mariah might have gone to work, and Myles had left his mother in the house alone.

"We'll check, just the same, and then we'll get the cows," Tanner said.

"If you didn't see her coming down the lane, my guess is she took the old trail through the woods. You know, the one, you boys, took all the time as a shortcut." Then Pap muttered. "Women didn't even have the sense to carry an umbrella. I gave her one of ours."

Well, that was something.

"I'll walk the trail. You drive over to the house and see if she reached home already," Tyler handed him the truck keys.

"I don't know why they keep leaving her alone if she can't

take care of herself." Pap frowned, the worry lines deepening on his forehead. "Maybe I should come help."

Tyler laid a hand on his grandfather's shoulder. "We got this, Pap. Just ensure there's a hot pot of coffee when we return."

They took off to find Mrs. Lehman.

Tanner forced himself to drive slowly. The sky had darkened with the storm. This constant trickle of rain that had started earlier in the day would worsen into the evening.

No one answered the door at the house, and Myles' truck sat out near the barn. He found the dapple-gray gelding in a stall with fresh bedding and hay. The horse nickered as he approached, someone had filled the hay rack not long ago, and the bucket hanging in the stall was two-thirds of the way full.

"Where did she go?"

Juniper pulled more hay out of the rack and ate.

"Thanks for the help."

Tanner walked to the edge of the barn. In the distance, he thought he could see something through the gloom of the fog gathering in the low areas of the field. He squinted, but the mist slithered through the trees.

A curl of smoke rose too high to be fog.

Someone had returned to the cabin.

"Momma!"

Mariah pulled the hood of her rain jacket down close. She tried to call Myles and got no answer.

She texted him and asked him to come to the house immediately, then deleted it the next second.

Emotions warred inside her while logic told her Momma couldn't have gone far. She checked everywhere in the house and left a note on the table for Myles.

She looked in the barn. No Momma there either.

Trudging up through the woods, she decided Momma would have gone to either the Evanses' place or the cabin. Dread swirled in her stomach.

Lord, help me find Momma. Let her be safe. And then she tossed in a quiet plea. *Not the cabin.*

It was closer. Mariah headed in that direction first. Second-guessing herself, she wondered if she should take the trail; it led to the Evanses' place but then cut partway and headed to the cabin. Would Momma stick to the path?

Had she put on anything more than her house slippers? Or a coat? What got in her mother's head to leave without saying a word? Either way, she would find her. "Momma!" she shouted up through the trees.

"I could use some help here," she muttered, rain slithering around the edge of her hood and dripping against her neck.

It didn't help to find footprints and made the leaves on the ground slippery and the ground beneath questionable. Good thing she left Juniper behind this time.

"Momma! Where are you?"

Somewhere in the distance, she heard someone shout, and she froze. Not Momma. The voice was too deep and drowned out by the heaviness of the falling drizzle. The air seemed to moisten her lungs as she drew a breath to call back and thought better of it.

It came again, and she quickened her pace.

Careful, Mariah. You don't know who else is in these woods.

She slipped over a cluster of rocks, trying to avoid a fallen tree in her way. She moved quickly through the forest on the narrow deer path they'd worn as kids. Nearly grown, a trace of the cleared area led the way.

She squinted to protect her eyes from the misting rain and clutched her cell phone in her pocket under her rain jacket. Too early to get dark. The storm clouds shifted in the sky and hid the sun from helping her in the dense foliage and fog.

The rain felt cold enough, landing on her face that snow would have been a blessing.

"Momma?" she called, not quite as loud, spotting the figure coming closer on the trail.

"Mariah?" Tyler Evans marched toward her, his shoulders hunched in and his head ducked to keep the mist off his face.

"What are you doing out here?" she asked, feeling surprised and defensive at the same time.

"Same thing as you. Pap said your mom came to the house. Tanner is headed to your place. We wanted to make sure she got home."

All the dread and worry in her started to seep away. "Tanner took Momma home?"

Tyler shook his head. "No. Sorry, that's not what I meant. He went there hoping she made it home. I came this way since Pap said she'd come this way to get to our place."

The false bottom of her hope dropped in her gut. "So, you don't know where Momma is? You didn't see her?"

"She didn't come home yet?"

Mariah tucked her hands in her pockets. She hadn't thought to grab gloves so that the cold drizzle wouldn't freeze her fingertips and send chills through her veins. "Would I be out here if she did?"

He tugged down on his beanie under the hood of his Carhart jacket. "We'll keep looking. Any ideas."

"One." Mariah glanced up to the bend where the trail cut and the cabin would lay ahead at the top of the hill. "Let's hope we find her before our unwanted company does first."

Tyler seemed to understand what she meant. Tanner must have explained it to him, and she tightened her fingers against her palms to try and warm them.

Had Tanner told Tyler everything? Or had he left out the part where he kissed her?

"Why don't you head back to the house in case she or

Tanner is there. I'll check the cabin, especially if there's company."

"My mom hasn't seen you in years. She might not know you and get frightened."

Unlike Tanner, his older brother had started to grow a beard, and with that beanie and jacket, he looked like a lumberjack out here in the forest.

"Right. Well, let's find her before it starts to storm. The winds are picking up. I can see your cheeks are pink with the cold." Tyler went ahead of her.

Was Tyler Evans hitting on her?

He'd always teased her when they were younger. No, not Tyler. He made more of a general observation than getting cute with her.

Her sense of smell had frozen in the chill of the rain, but her other senses worked fine.

The closer they got to the cabin, the slower Tyler moved. Above them, lightning blinked on the dark gray horizon. She tried not to cringe, waiting for the boom to follow. It came a second later, and Tyler glanced back at her.

"Okay?"

She nodded.

"Better move into the trees more. We're going to get caught in the downpour."

A loud roaring came through the forest. Not thunder or the storm. Mariah heard the four-wheelers before she saw them. Blurs of color retreated down through the trees.

Tyler took off in a jog, and Mariah headed toward the cabin. It was dark inside, but someone had most definitely been here. Smoke, thick and white, curled from the chimney.

Not taking the chance it could be Momma in there, she found the front door locked. She moved the key to a new hiding place under a window seal.

Broken glass greeted her. No wonder they didn't need a key. They'd broken one of the windows. Momma wouldn't have done that. She would have looked in the old spot for the key if she remembered.

Mariah pulled out her phone. Her hands shook, and she managed to take a picture of the broken window. They hadn't even bothered to put it the rest of the way down after they used it to gain entrance.

Tyler came up through the woods.

Rumbling warnings from the sky signaled mother nature's intentions.

She took the key, unlocked the door, and sucked in her breath in the darkness of what little light spilled in behind the cabin door. She turned on the flashlight on her phone, instantly wishing she hadn't.

"So much for cleaning the place up."

"You can report the break-in when we get back to your place. Tanner texted. Your mom and Myles are back at the house."

Then she noticed Tanner had sent her a message as well.

"Myles must have got my message and come home."

Tyler rubbed his chin. "Either way, I'll walk the rest of the way to your place and grab a ride with Tanner. The storm is coming in, and we should get moving."

Thank you, Lord. Momma was safe.

13

Once Mariah got past the barn, she ran the rest of the way to the house. Tyler closed the gate as he followed in a fast walk.

Tanner sat in an old wicker chair on the porch.

Catching her breath, she asked, "Where is Momma?"

"In the house with Myles." He stood.

Just then, the sky sounded like a whip snapping and opening up, pelleting them with heavy rain. "You could have waited inside."

"So now I'm welcome?" He lifted a brow.

"Come in. Both of you." She turned and motioned for Tyler to come, too. "You'll need a good cup of coffee to ward off the chill after being in the rain."

Tyler stepped up on the porch. "I'll take it."

Other than Pap's black wakeup juice, Tanner hadn't had a good cup of coffee in ages. "You sure Myles won't mind? He wasn't thrilled to encounter me on the trail. I came upon him and your mom about halfway up to the cabin."

Mariah opened the door, holding it for the two brothers. "I don't care at this moment. I need to see Momma and make sure she's okay. You don't want to go back out in this rain without warming up first. You'll freeze with the wind and the downpour."

Neither man argued with her. However, the exchanged look between the two brothers didn't escape her attention either.

It was a cup of coffee to warm their insides. They'd gone looking for Momma without her having to ask them. It was the least she could do.

Inside, she stepped past the men. She shed her wet jacket and invited them to do the same. She glanced around the living room, not seeing Momma when Myles appeared. His hair was tousled and damp. He seemed to have come straight from a hot shower. A dark gash bled at his cheek, and his left eye swelled. The flesh around it darkened with the onset of a bruise. He held his hand to his ribs and scowled at her.

"What happened? Where is Momma?"

"She's in her room," he grunted.

"Momma never goes in her room." Mariah tilted her head, looking at Myles suspiciously.

"She does when I put her there." Myles moved slowly past her.

Mariah went to her mother's room and found her mother curled up on the bed, weeping. "Momma?"

Her mother glanced over at her. "Mariah. Where did you go? I was afraid those bad men got you!"

Momma moved fast, grabbing Mariah and wrapping her in her arms. "Don't you ever go away like that without telling me first!"

"I won't. I didn't go anywhere. I was here. You're the one who left the house."

"It's those Evans boys. I told old Silas. Poor things don't got a mother. Somebody has to give them a good straightening out. No wonder Mark's got an attitude! I don't want you running off with them no more, you hear!"

Mariah held onto her mother, relieved to find her safe and in one piece.

She let her mother scold her, ground her, and warn her. Meanwhile, Mariah helped her mother into dry clothes and ensured she wouldn't catch a cold.

"I'll get you some hot tea, and we'll have a bowl of hot soup tonight for supper."

Her mother didn't respond. Mariah led her mother back out into the living room, knowing how being in her room agitated more than soothed her these days.

In the kitchen, she heard the men talking. Myles' voice was grating and mean. She hurried out to make peace. Myles stood by the sink, a pack of peas against his face. "I told them to get out."

"And I told him we weren't leaving until we made sure everything was all right with your mom," Tyler said, crossing his arms and standing by the kitchen door.

"I've still got your brother's permission to kick your butt when you're out of line."

Myles lifted his lip in a sneer. Whoever had punched him had missed his mouth and hit his eye instead.

"You have nerve coming here," Myles grunted. "Both of you."

"I invited them in." Mariah pushed Myles away from the sink to make room to fill the coffee pot.

"You'd let a murderer in our house?" Myles asked, his voice harsh. "He killed our brother, Mariah."

"I know." No one understood her brother's pain more than she did. "He also brought Momma home when you should have been here with her. And where have you been today?"

Myles' nostrils flared. His good eye narrowed on her. "None of your business."

"He's right," Tanner spoke up. "We should go. Pap's waiting for us."

"Be careful. The rain is coming down hard."

Tyler grabbed his jacket. "Glad your mom is home safe." Shoving his hands in his pockets, he made a face. Pulling out a clear bag from within, he held it out to Mariah. "You're a nurse, right? You can take these to the hospital and dispose of them, can't you?"

"You don't need them?" Mariah took the zip lock bag from him.

"I found them and figured it best to dispose of them properly. I don't want them falling into the wrong hands."

"You called Mr. Yeager?" Tanner asked.

"I did. He doesn't know."

Mariah moved the capsules around in the clear bag. "Where did you find these?"

She bit the inside of her lip, waiting for Tyler's response.

"He probably stole them," Myles huffed.

"They were in between the feed sacks when we were unloading them. They yours?" Tanner asked.

Myles' stiffened. "No. Sure they're not his?"

"I know what these are." She rubbed the pills between the plastic to hold calm. "Momma takes the same ones."

Myles shoved off the sink and headed into the living room. She watched him go in and sink on the couch, stretching out.

"Who are you fighting with now?" Momma asked.

"No one. Leave me alone, Momma."

"Where did you get hurt, Mark?"

"I'm not Mark! Now, leave me alone."

"Don't you think I know my boys apart? Now let me see that eye, Mark Allen Lehman."

"I'm Myles." He made a noise in his throat, got up, and headed for the stairs.

Momma started to follow him. "Myles?"

Mariah moved to the doorway between the kitchen and living room. "That's right, Momma. That's Myles. Just leave him be. I'll check on him in a bit."

She'd check to make sure nothing in his brain had gotten rattled. Hoping he might open up and tell her what happened without anyone else around, she sighed at Momma's stunned face.

Upstairs, Myles' bedroom door slammed.

"He's all grown up," Momma said.

"Yeah. He is." Or he thought he was.

Mariah heard the screen door and left Momma there, staring at the stairs. She followed Tanner and Tyler out on the porch.

"I'll take care of these."

"I appreciate that," Tyler bumped Tanner. "This isn't letting up. We best make a run for it." Tyler rushed to the truck, but Tanner lingered.

"We should probably talk." She shivered as the wind brought the rain in on the porch. Tanner moved to shield her. "About those pills or what happened earlier today?"

"Both."

"I didn't steal your mother's pills."

She took his hand and squeezed it, reassuring him. "The thought hadn't occurred to me, and I'd appreciate it if you didn't go trying to turn this on my brother."

Tanner's thumb swept over the top of her hand in a circular motion. "Only if you'll do me a favor and ask him about working at the feed mill."

Don't trust him, Mariah. Don't trust him.

She slipped her hand away. "I should probably go back inside before Momma decides to go up the stairs and upset them both more."

"If you need me to come back later to check on her while you're at work, you know how to get a hold of me."

Tyler beeped the horn from the truck.

"I'm off tonight. We'll be good."

He leaned in. Mariah's breath hitched, but then Tyler honked the horn, and Tanner hurried to get through the rain.

She watched as the two Evans brothers pulled out of the yard. Hugging herself, she waited until the lights of the truck disappeared. Lightning rippled in the sky, and the winds sent cold rain splattering against her face.

Momma's pills were clutched in her fist.

Please, Lord, let it not be so.

Mariah fell asleep on the couch. Myles had locked his door and refused to let her check his injuries. She stayed up most of the night with Momma, binge-watching old episodes of Grey's Anatomy.

Sometime in the early morning hours, Myles had slipped past her. He didn't bother to leave a note or text her where he was going.

She slept in later than usual. Myles left his door open, and her heart sank, seeing he'd packed up enough of his things for her to notice.

It wouldn't last. He would come back.

Her phone rang, and Matt's agitated voice greeted her.

"How nice of you to call," she said, heading to the kitchen for coffee.

"What's going on?" Now he called her and asked.

She debated dumping out the leftover liquid from last night to make new or taking her chances with the brew there.

What was there won.

Desperate moments of needing caffeine and dealing with her brother caved to her better judgment.

"I figured Jess would tell you." She poured a cup and placed it in the microwave. Their whole lives had taken place in this kitchen. She held onto the phone, watching the microwave count down until her brew got hot enough to drink.

Outside, she peered at the bleak gray horizon, the damp

grass, and the rain-soaked trees. She could hear the wind rattling the chimes on the porch.

"Myles came to see me this morning. He's moving in with a friend. What is going on?"

That was the second time he asked her that.

She heard a truck and thought maybe Myles had returned. Had he forgotten something? She glanced out the window, spotting Tanner getting out of the truck.

Great, just what she needed.

"What did Myles tell you?" She couldn't wait for the coffee to heat up. She hit the CANCEL button and pulled it out, lukewarm at best.

She drank while Matt spoke, gulping it down fast while keeping an eye on Tanner coming to the house.

"He's tired of you being his mother. You got to stop trying to control his life, Mariah. You're not in charge here."

Like Matt was? She kept that thought to herself.

She finished the coffee, not usually one to drink it black, and took a deep breath inhaling the last of the dark rich scent. Daddy always drank it black. It made her wince.

"Well, then you can handle Myles. I have to go." She hung up on her brother and headed to the door before Tanner could knock.

"What do you want now, Evans?"

Tanner frowned at her.

Okay, her voice sounded an octave or two on the highly irate side.

She crossed her arms. A girl could have a bad morning once in a while. The coffee cup was still in her hand, dangling from her fingers. She needed more of something. Of what, she couldn't be sure. Time? For the caffeine to kick in?

He looked so downright put together in those laced-up work boots and hip-hugging jeans in the morning. He pulled a beanie cap down over his head to shield the winds from knocking him in the ears. She refused to invite him in.

Last evening, she had hours to think of what had happened, and none of it made sense. Or the conclusions she wouldn't allow her mind to reach.

"I guess that answers that." He turned away, headed to step down off the porch.

"Wait," she shouldn't be taking out her foul mood on him. Not yet, anyway. Not entirely sure who was the guiltier party in all this. Him? She wanted to blame all this on Tanner. And deep down, she couldn't because neither her conscience nor her heart would allow her.

"What do you want?" she said in a gentler, more exasperated than annoyed way.

He put his hands in his coat pocket and faced her. "Figured we might have that chat, you know, talk about what happened."

"This isn't a good time." Never would be the better option. Her face flushed a little. From the caffeine hitting her bloodstream and not the memory of kissing Tanner, or so she tried to push it back in her mind.

It was best they both forgot.

Nothing could ever happen between them. Not after what Tanner had done. How could he expect her to move on like nothing ever happened?

Something had happened, alright.

Tanner Evans had happened.

That kiss had been a mistake. One Mariah wouldn't ever erase from her memory, along with the one of him abandoning her that night and of her momma's cries and her brother's funeral.

"I can come back. You let me know when."

She swallowed the emotions lumping in her throat. Quickly her mind raced for a retort, something sassy and a little sharp to keep Tanner from getting the wrong idea between them.

"I don't think that's a good idea."

Which only made his face pinch together. "You plan to avoid me and forget it happened." He shook his head. "We need to talk about it. I get you might need more time. A lot is happening. I just want you to know I'm here and not going anywhere."

Same old Tanner.

She had always admired that about him.

Envied him at times. The way he offered to help when no one else had.

She always suspected it was him, and not Mark, who did Mark's chores in the barn for them to run off when their father gave them things to do.

And here he stood, more life worn and battered than she, offering support even when he knew he wasn't welcome. God had a funny way of sending a sign to her.

Frankly, they would all have to learn to cope with things. Whatever that kiss had been about would have to wait. From her side, it was an impulsive desire she couldn't afford to repeat a second time. No matter how much she wanted to lean into him, feel his warmth, and press her lips to his for a repeat performance.

Tanner Evans had been the first boy she wanted to kiss. He might not have been the first, and he couldn't be her last. He couldn't be her anything, which shook her to her core.

He needed to leave.

Mariah had bigger problems. Ones he helped bring to her family. And she was about to tell him when in the distance, a gunshot echoed from beyond the trees.

14

"Tanner."

She'd been about to say something to him, but only his name escaped her lips. Her eyes widened as she glanced in the direction of the noise.

"It sounded like it came from the direction of the cabin."

"That can't be good."

He gripped her cold hand in his warm one. "Stay here, and I'll go check it out."

"It could be hunters," She held on to him, giving him pause. Her facial expression had softened, and he could swear he saw concern in her eyes. Was this the woman who, a moment before, looked like she was building up to tell him off?

"It's too early, and aren't your lands posted?" She did care. Even if she didn't want to admit it. A flicker of hope gave him some confidence.

Mariah nodded. "Yours, too, right?"

"I'll check it out and be back," he looked her in the eyes. "And, we will talk."

He squeezed her hand, trying to warm them and assure her. They had things to settle. He wouldn't let her push him away this easily.

Tanner made a terrible mistake in his life, but he decided last night he wouldn't allow it to define him or his future. He cared too much about Mariah not to try. He had a lifetime to prove it, no matter how long or short God granted him to live.

"I'll come with you. If it's on my land, I should know about it."

"Your mother?"

"She's taking her mid-morning nap. Just wait a second while I lock the doors and set the alarms."

Tanner shook his head. "Too much time. I'll come back."

She probably didn't hear him racing into the house. He couldn't wait for her, not if he wanted a chance to catch who made that shot.

A second shot jolted him into the action, not as far in the distance as the first.

He took off to his truck, speeding out of the yard and down the drive. He headed for the cabin lane, his heart racing along with the man singing on the radio—some moaning cowboy who lost his love and needed a dime.

Pap's truck skidded in the mud of the lane. He weaved and kicked in the four-wheel drive. Halfway up the lane, his truck spun to make it up the hill, and he swerved, taking it off-road, driving into the woods as far as he could until he had no choice but to get out and go on foot.

There was no one at the cabin.

Tanner pulled out his phone and kept hold of it as he trudged farther up, not finding any signs of anyone around.

A few no-trespassing signs greeted him along the way.

He scouted around and walked the fence line when he heard the sounds of something behind him.

Tanner made a fist and sighed. Mariah rode toward him on her dapple-gray gelding.

They'd have heard the gelding snorting and moving across the damp turf if anything had been here.

"I told you to stay."

"This is my land. You can't stop me from being on it," she said.

Here they went again. "Then get back on your land, Lehman. You've crossed the property line." He pointed to the fence, and she scowled.

"You could have waited for me."

"You could have stayed at the house, and I would have come back," he grabbed hold of the high-tension wire, knowing it wouldn't be electrified, and slipped between the strands.

He squinted and looked out into the distance. Cows. What were they doing in this field? Tyler must have moved them to get them out of the muck of the barn after last night's storm. He could have put them somewhere closer when they cleaned the main shed.

A few were lying down.

"You? Come back? I'm not stupid enough to fall for that again." Mariah dismounted and led Juniper closer. The gelding didn't like the idea of getting close to the fence. The horse held his ground a few feet from the high-tension wire.

"Listen."

Tanner listened.

They would cross the bridge of their past later.

Hearing nothing, he shook his head.

"I thought I heard something."

"Hibernating squirrels?"

Did squirrels hibernate in early October? Maybe they'd both grown paranoid with all the events of the past couple of weeks.

"I'm going to go check on the cows. If someone is out here hunting, I might have to move them back across the road and closer to the barn."

"I'll help."

One moment the woman wanted to get rid of him. A moment later, she helped him. She needed to make up her mind.

She confused him.

She was Mark's little sister.

They all needed to move on.

He pressed on a strand of the fence. High tension usually didn't budge much, but he wanted to show her it was safe to slide between the wires.

Once when they were younger, Mark and Tanner had tricked her into touching a piece of a live wire. It shocked her. The hot current had left a tiny scar across the lifeline on her palm where it burned.

He never agreed with Mark for them to do that and found it least funny between them when Mariah had gone crying back to the farmhouse and Mrs. Lehman's arms.

He'd caused her pain back then, too.

It seemed inevitable between them.

She took the hand he offered as she righted herself. It took an act of balance and skill to slip through while staying on one's feet.

On the other side, Juniper stood, ground tied.

"He be alright, like that?"

Mariah glanced back over at the horse. "He'll stay there as long as he can see me."

Satisfied with her response, he walked toward the cows. She took her hand back from his, and he tried to ignore her, letting go. He had always admired her stubborn streak. It gave her strength and courage that had no doubt carried her through the challenging years in his absence.

You shouldn't have gone this way, Mark's irritated voice echoed in his head, and he shook it away.

I know what I'm doing.

Out of habit, he started counting the cows. Most had clustered in a grove of trees while a handful grazed out in the more open area, and several laid down.

Too much quiet echoed around them. He could hear the cows chewing their cud, and the grass smelled odd. Maybe it was the air, for, after a good rain, things smelled like dew and that freshness that one couldn't explain.

It distracted him, and he lost count. He counted again, stopping and turning in a circle. Two were missing. He counted again, walking a little farther. They could have gone anywhere. It wasn't like a cow to stray from the rest of the herd unless she had calved and the others left her alone.

"Tanner."

She touched his arm, tugging a bit on the excess of his canvas sleeve. "Did you count?"

"I'm missing two."

"Are you sure?"

"No. I can check with Pap."

"You might want to check over there," Mariah pointed to where a cow lay on its side. The neck stretched out, its head pointed up, and its legs straight out.

A young Holstein heifer lay dead. Its eyes were blank and black to the world. Tanner crouched beside it, "Well, we know what one of the shots was."

Mariah knelt beside him, seemingly not noticing the dampness of the earth seeping into her jeans. "They probably missed the first time."

Her words needled him. "Or shot this one twice."

"You going to help me flip her over to find out?" Mariah ran her hand down over the cow's stiff neck to the animal's chest, where blood bloomed bright red against the white.

"Hit the heart?"

"I'm a nurse, not a veterinarian, but your heifer is dead."

Tanner snorted, more to let out frustration than Mariah's declaration.

"I'm a farmer. I could have told you that."

It sent a faint smile across her lips. Tanner stood up and looked out over the herd. "One is still missing."

"Let's hope it got spooked and is in hiding in another grove of trees."

"Or it's dead," he had to face facts.

"You should call the Sheriff." She rose to stand beside him. He noticed how she turned away from the sight of the cow. Her hands stuffed into her jacket. So cold. He should warm them, but he needed to make that call first.

"You should go back to Juniper before he gets restless. I don't know if he can see you this far out."

"I'll ride around the fence row. If I spot anything, I'll let you know."

Someone shot his cow. A second one was missing. He glanced at his phone; he figured he wouldn't have cell service. "No. This is my problem. I'll handle it."

"It seems it is both our problems."

He couldn't risk anything happening to her. "You should go home. Is Myles with your mom?"

He hadn't seen the truck when he pulled in.

She bit her lip. Now, who was sending who away? He hated letting her go, but it was the safest option. "Text me when you're in the house."

"I'll think about it," she marched away. After a distance, she paused and glanced over her shoulder at him.

"Tanner. I'm sorry."

Her words seeped into him, warm and comforting with a hint of remorse.

Mariah called off work that evening and the next. The worst thing about working at a hospital is you had to have a doctor's excuse to prove you were sick.

She used up all her vacation days, and Jess sympathetically suggested Mariah call Woodside to admit Momma. Of course, she should have expected the suggestion from Matt's wife.

She'd hoped Jess would see Momma needed to be at home.

Even in the few days Mariah had stayed home and made sure Momma had taken her medication properly, Mariah had seen a positive difference in her mother.

They played card games one afternoon while the rain came down in buckets.

Last evening, they'd stayed up late kneading bread and baking it the old-fashion way. Momma hadn't wanted to make bread in years.

It lifted her spirits since Tanner stayed away.

Mariah often listened for a vehicle in the lane, hoping for Myles to finish blowing his steam and come home or for Tanner to be standing on her front porch.

She'd expected it from Myles.

She shouldn't have expected it from Tanner.

"When those boys come back over, you send a loaf with them," Momma said.

By 'boys,' she meant Tyler and Tanner.

"I don't think they'll be coming back anytime soon." It bothered her not to see him. Tanner Evans had always been trouble with a capital "T."

She learned a long time ago not to trust him on his word.

She texted him to say she got home against her better judgment.

He hadn't had the courtesy to reply.

What had she expected? For him to show up and tell her if he found the missing cow? For the sheriff to show up and ask her questions because she'd heard the shots and technically had been the one to spot the cow first?

Had he forgotten he wanted to talk? Did that kiss mean something to him?

They had enough bread to get them through a week, so she froze some.

Momma looked at her curiously, "What's the matter?"

"Nothing," Mariah mumbled.

Momma put a hand on her hip and gave her a more in-depth look. "You should have been racing out this door by now to take that bread over to Silas." Momma's eyes narrowed. "You find some other boy to chase after you haven't told me about?"

Surprised, her mother had noticed that. Not that it mattered. "That was a long time ago."

"If you say so," Momma washed dishes in the sink, more alert today and in a bright, cheery mood.

Her heart stuttered a bit at the sound of her phone ringing. Dread squeezed her at the sight of the hospital's number on her screen. She had to take this call.

"Hello?" Lord forgive her. She let her voice go weak and hoped they'd hear the sickness in it. Not that anything was physically ailing her.

"Mariah," Gail's voice sounded on the phone. "I hate to do this to you, but I need you to come in early tonight."

"Me?" Mariah sank into a chair at the table.

"What's wrong?" her mother asked.

Mariah waved her off. "Can't it be someone else?"

"Nope. Harrison said it had to be you. And if you don't show, you go. Out. Permanently."

"I know what go means." How did she go when Myles was gone, and she hadn't found anyone to stay with Momma?

"I'm sorry. How are you feeling?"

Oh, right. She was sick. "Doesn't matter. Myles left, and I don't know what to do."

There was silence on the line for a bit. "I don't know what

to tell you. I've been praying for you, and I know things are hard. But you need to show up for your shift."

"I'll figure it out."

"Did you try one of those home health services?"

"We're too far out of town for them to come," Mariah sighed.

"What about your other brother?"

"I told you. Matt will use any excuse to put Momma in a home."

Gail remained silent.

"I'll see you in a bit." Or not. Mariah disconnected the call.

Lord, what do I do?

She needed this job.

She needed to stay with Momma.

Mariah buried her head in her hands. There had to be a way.

Her mother patted her on the shoulder. "There, there. Everything always works out for the best in the end."

She had to believe it did. Otherwise, she might crumble. Mariah stared at her phone as her mother headed into the living room.

Her life revolved around Momma and the hospital.

She didn't have many friends.

Mariah hadn't been to church in a while because of her work schedule.

A little voice whispered in her head, *Was this best for Momma? For her?*

At that moment, it felt like the whole world was against her.

Something inside her gave her a little push, and Tanner's number lay under the tap of her finger. Could she trust him?

Did she have a choice?

Maybe this once.

"Momma? Is it okay if Tanner comes over?"

"I don't want no trouble," Momma said.

"No, Momma." She answered as she did when she was younger. "No trouble."

Except, her whole life seemed to have become one trouble after the next. With a capital "T."

15

Tanner made breakfast and a hot pot of coffee for when Mariah got home. Nervous, he didn't know if she'd want caffeine or to eat. If it were him, Tanner would have gone straight to bed, but Mariah had never been the predictable type. Or at least not this new Mariah he'd come to know.

Each, in their way, gained a sense of responsibility, and it lit something inside him far more than admiration or respect.

He'd tell her if she gave him a chance.

Mrs. Lehman had cooked her own breakfast, while Tanner stayed out of her way, watchful while she worked. He turned off the stove when she forgot and listened as a game show host shouted from the television in the corner of the living room.

He had a cup ready and a plate as Mariah came home.

"You're here?"

She acted surprised.

"You asked me to stay here with your mother. I am here."

"Yeah, but…" she sputtered for words. "Don't you have to go milk the cows?"

"Tyler and Pap took care of it this morning. I'll have to be there this evening for sure."

"Oh," she said.

"You look exhausted. Rough night?"

Because every woman wanted to hear, she appeared haggard first thing in the morning. He had yet to gain experience in this department. He would have to work on his morning social skills.

"Not that you don't look good in those scrubs."

She lifted a brow, her cheeks going a little pink.

Okay, he'd shut up.

"I hope you made all that for you because I'm tired, and I need to sleep. Please make sure you lock the door so the alarm turns on."

"Of course." Everything he had to tell her could wait.

"Was she okay?"

"She got a little peeved at first, telling me Mark wasn't here and asking me when I was going home. I told her I was here for a sleepover, and she said it was okay. That seemed to pacify her. I stayed in the kitchen, reading a book to keep an eye on her."

"You didn't sleep?"

"I crashed on your couch when she was sleeping. If she noticed me, she didn't say anything. She made her breakfast about an hour ago."

Mariah rubbed the back of her neck. Tanner moved behind her and placed his hands on her shoulders to ease the tension. She stiffened, then relaxed as he pressed his thumbs into the knots that had formed there.

Standing close to her, Tanner could smell the passion fruit scent of her shampoo and the faint antiseptics from the hospital. He leaned in more than he should have, and she stiffened. "I remember you helped your dad. I figured you'd do something here on the farm or in business. You never spoke of being a nurse."

"And you wanted to build cars with my brother, but then you caused the accident that killed him." Her voice trailed off; a new knot formed between her shoulder blades.

Faster man. Faster!

Tanner released her and stepped back. He couldn't make Mark's voice ever go away.

One tragic event changed both of their lives.

She turned, her shoulder brushing his arm. "You're pale. I shouldn't have said that. Do you need to sit down? I can't help myself from speaking what's on my mind sometimes."

Yeah, it was one of the other things he liked about her.

"I suppose it comes with having brothers. I never learned to sugarcoat things, but what you did, Tanner. It's—."

"Unforgivable." He finished for her.

"I was going to say it was hard for all of us. I lost my brother and my best friend when Mark died. My parents talked about suing yours, but my father didn't. I think it was because of my mother. She said the money wouldn't bring Mark back and would only bring more grief."

She paused. "I hated you for the longest time. You had no intention of coming back that night. You and Mark did anything you could to ditch me."

Her chest rose and fell with the depth of her words. Tanner caused her this pain—her and her family.

"And I live with it every day. There isn't a time I don't pray when I slide behind the wheel to drive. I see him, hear him. A few counselors in prison told me it was guilt, not Mark, and I needed to stop feeling guilty. I've never told Tyler or even Pap about it. People would think I'm crazy."

He waited for her reaction. She nodded. "I don't think you're crazy. I hear him sometimes, too, memories of things he would say. There's nothing wrong with holding on to memories as long as you don't allow the grief to consume you. You're not the only one who needs counseling. Matt refused to go. Momma's mind started slipping. She would forget Mark wasn't with us, and then it got worse as the years passed."

"It's not your fault." Tanner got the impression she blamed her mother's condition on herself. "Blame me if it makes you feel better. I am used it."

"I already did, but I blamed myself more. I couldn't save him, even though I heard my parents talking about how Mark bled out. No one saw he'd cut his foot under the dash panel. It took too long for the responder to get to him."

"He tried stepping on the pedal to make us go faster. Angie had left with a bunch of others, and he wanted to catch up. I saw her in the backseat with another guy. I knew what would happen when we got there, and it was safer to leave you behind. I had every intention of coming back."

"It doesn't matter."

He could see the weariness in her. This shouldn't have been the time or the place. He had other things he needed to tell her. One thing he knew that would upset her in their present situation.

"It matters to me. When I saw you by the campfire, head bent with another guy, I knew I had to get back, but I couldn't let Mark go on his own either."

Tanner touched Mariah's cheek. His stomach twisting, he said, "We were trapped in that car for a while until they found us. We talked, and I tried to make him laugh. I blacked out a few times, but Mark made me promise to look out for you. He knew what I didn't."

Tears streamed down her face. "Why are you telling me this?"

"Because I care about you. I don't want to see you hurt or anyone else in your family. This is why I have to tell you some things that will upset you more."

Mariah sniffled. "What things?"

Tanner pulled her in, surprised she'd allow him to hug her close. She fit into his embrace, and he savored the warmth of holding her. For all he knew, it might be the last time she would allow him to get this close again.

"A woman came by. She left her card. She's a social worker from the county. She got a tip that your momma was here alone."

"I'm not surprised. I figured it would happen sooner or later."

She pulled away from him. Wiping her tears, she moved over by the counter and sagged against it. "I'll take care of it."

Determination lit on her face, and he exhaled, keeping his distance. It was just the emotions of reliving the accident and the relief of getting it off his chest.

She didn't hate him entirely. She didn't love him either.

He cared far too much for her to admit it when she needed to recover from a long night at the hospital.

"Well, I better go. You're tired, and I have things to tend to at the farm." Everything else could wait for another time. He wouldn't burden her with more, especially when they'd both been bared and vulnerable for a moment.

He drank in the view of her, as it might be the last sight of her for a while. She might think differently of him after she rested and processed their conversation.

"It's not like Myles not to come home after school," Momma remarked as Mariah finished cleaning up after their dinner. "I wonder where that boy has gone!"

"He's at Matt's house, Momma. He's not going to be coming home."

Momma frowned, and Mariah could see the cloud of confusion hooding over her mother's eyes. "I don't know Matt. Is that a new boy at school?"

She'd been worse the past two days. Without Myles coming home, it unbalanced their mother's already delicate tightrope of walking between the past and the present.

"Matt is your firstborn. He's your son, too."

It hadn't been a good day or the end of a good week. She'd called around to find a sitter for Momma. Thus far, no services had availability, and one said they could come in to do the paperwork in about three weeks. Unless something opened up sooner, Mariah would have no choice but to rely on Tanner for assistance. She offered to pay him, and surprisingly he accepted.

He knew better than to argue with her.

It also made it feel less like a personal favor, and more like a professional relationship because heaven forbid she become friends with him again.

Deep down in that hollow space that opened inside her and created a void in her life when Mark died, Tanner Evans still lived. He would have come back for her. But, more than that, it had been a terrible accident. Only God knew what happened inside that vehicle after they crashed. And God help her, she believed Tanner. Mark had been the ringleader of many of their escapades, often leading them into trouble.

And trouble had a way of following her family ever since.

Mariah couldn't fill that void to keep from thinking about him. Although she had bigger worries and no time for relationships, they seemed to find her. She shouldn't be encouraging Tanner to keep coming around.

She'd almost about gotten that kiss evaporated from her system. Almost.

After helping Momma shower and get her settled with a game show on television, Mariah left Tanner a plate of double chocolate brownies and went out to sit on the front porch. There wouldn't be many days left for sitting outside and watching the evening sun send dark, bold, golden streamers through the horizon.

A dark red SUV pulled down the lane and parked in the yard. Mariah kept her jacket pulled tighter around her, waiting. She hadn't called the social worker from the card Tanner had given her, hoping the woman would simply not bother to come back. She rose and stepped off the porch.

A man stepped out of the vehicle. He was average height, with a faded logo T-shirt and black boots laced up over his jeans. He had a tattoo on his neck, peeking up from around his collarbone. As he approached, she could make out the tips of an inked wing.

He had a few days of growth on his chin, and despite his grin, those dark eyes bleed around the irises.

"What can I do for you?" she crossed her arms. Any moment Tanner would come for her to leave and go to work.

"You're Myles' sister." His grin wavered; those eyes narrowed.

Mariah pulled back her shoulders, going into nurse mode. "Who wants to know?"

He reached up and scratched the scruff on his jaw. "A friend. He owes me, and so do you."

"I don't know what you mean."

The man walked toward her. Mariah backed up until her heels came in contact with the porch stairs. He extended a foot on the porch beside her and leaned on his leg to get close. "I know you work at the hospital. I also know you're a Special K girl."

"You're wrong." She held still. Even in a small town like Hidden Hills, the reference to a street drug hadn't alluded to her. "There's no Special K here."

A muscle in his neck jumped at the tattoo. "You took something from me. I want it back."

Mariah balled her hands into a fist to keep from fleeing. She glanced at the house, hearing her heartbeat thudding in her ears.

Any moment, Tanner. She prayed for him to pull into the yard in his pap's old truck.

"You should talk to the police. I'm sure they'll be interested to know it was yours."

Lightning quick, he grabbed her arm. "I get my stash back, or I guess you're going to have to get some cash and some narcotics to replace it. With. Interest."

His breath reeked of nicotine and barbecue. She held her breath to stop being sick. "I don't have access to either."

"Fifty k Nursie, and I've got a lot of pain right now. Not as much as what your momma will be in if my people start feeling the withdrawal. And you can tell that brother of yours not to be late with his next payment."

"Stay away from my family and keep away from the cabin."

"Or what?" He tilted his head, his hand reaching for her face, and she jerked back. His grin widened. "Three days. No cops. No farm boy from next door."

Is that why Tanner hadn't shown? Had something else happened? To Tanner? To one of the Evans. She tried to breathe in short breaths. She was an emergency room nurse; Mariah had trained to handle all kinds of hostile situations for dealing with patients.

"You're out of your mind if you think I will get drugs from the hospital for you."

He grabbed her by the hair, and she cried out.

Her hands flew back, struggling to get him to release her.

Tyler's truck pulled down the lane and came into the yard.

Alarm spread through her.

"Three days." He released her.

Tanner jumped out of the truck.

The man strode to his SUV. "You take good care of that mother of yours, you hear?"

Fury gathered in Tanner's face, and she rushed to him, colliding with him as the man got in the SUV.

"Who was that? What did he want?"

"He's a friend of Myles." She hadn't realized she was clinging to him until his arm came around her. He watched as the SUV pulled out of the yard and back down the lane.

"What did he want?"

She took a moment to slow her heart and collect her thoughts. *Oh Lord, what has Myles gotten involved in?*

"Where's your truck?" she asked.

"That's not important. We can talk about that later."

Later. She grabbed her phone and looked at the time.

"You're late! I'm going to be late! I can't be late!" She raced to the porch, grabbed her purse, and took off toward her car.

Sounds of the engine trying to turn over made her throat close. *God no! I can't lose my job.*

She could picture Dr. Harrison standing at the nurses' station, watching the seconds tick to the hour for an excuse to turn her into Human Resources and yank her livelihood from her.

She pounded the steering wheel. "Start!"

Tanner tapped on the window, her chest heaving as the adrenaline rush from the tattooed creep sent her system into overload. She trembled with the force of it, transmitting cold in her veins. She would lose her job, for sure.

"Take the truck." Tanner held out his keys to her as she opened the door.

"It's too late. I can't get there on time."

"You won't if you keep sitting here. Take the truck. It's not like I'm going anywhere until you get back."

"Won't Tyler mind?"

"He's got Pap's truck. Go and stop arguing before you're late." Tanner pointed toward the truck.

Mariah swallowed any more words of protest. Grabbing her bag, she headed for Tyler's truck.

"Mariah," Tanner pressed the keys in her hand. "Promise you won't go speeding. I know you're in a hurry, but no job is worth your life."

Those eyes that expression warmed her in places that lay

dormant for too long. She took the keys. "Don't worry. I'll bring back Tyler's truck in one piece."

"It's not the truck I'm worried about."

And before she could protest, Tanner planted a kiss on her lips. It ended as fast as it started. Mariah drove in a daze. *Lord, please help her get to work on time and in one piece.*

16

Sounds of someone going up the stairs called Tanner out of his light sleep. He dozed on the couch, falling asleep a little after midnight to the sounds of Mrs. Lehman's snores. Groggily, he checked the time on his phone lying on the coffee table.

Almost five in the morning.

He sat up, trying not to disturb the older woman in the chair. She preferred Robert's old recliner to the bedroom downstairs.

He listened and heard the sounds of someone moving around upstairs. He got up, grabbed his phone, and went to investigate. "Mariah?" He whispered up the stairs.

A moment later, Myles came stomping down the tread-worn stairs.

"What are you doing here?" He didn't mean it the way it blurted out. Mariah told him Myles had gone to stay with Matt.

"I live here," Myles jumped down the last two stairs and shouldered past Tanner. "Get out of my house."

"I will once Mariah comes."

"Her car is here. Where is she?" Myles had a duffle bag and a jacket in one hand.

His hair was mussed, and he stunk like stale alcohol. Dark rings and the yellowing of an old bruise on his cheekbone made his face look hollow, and his eyes sunk in.

"Car wouldn't start. So I let her take the truck. You know you look like crap, man. You okay?"

"This is your fault. Going where you don't belong, and having Mariah call the cops. Now you're in our house. Get out!" Myles dropped his duffle bag and heaved out his chest. The younger man glared at him.

"Don't shout. You'll wake and upset your mother."

"Good. Maybe they'll finally come and take her away," Myles kicked his bag toward the door. "And they'll come for you."

Tanner ran his hand down his face.

Myles had been nine when Mark died. Could a kid grow up with such bitterness and hate inside him? Deep inside, Tanner figured he could.

He met guys in prison who took the wrong path for the wrong reasons, having justified their actions as victims of broken homes and traumatic events as children.

This wasn't a path Tanner wanted to see Myles head down. But, feeling obligated to him as a friend and almost brotherly, Tanner said, "Is that what you want? Your mom to go away? You'd miss her."

Myles crossed his arms. "I told you to get out."

Tanner moved over by the counter in the kitchen, trying to draw Myles away from disturbing Mrs. Lehman. "I'll leave when Mariah tells me to leave."

"You mean when you kill her? Like you killed our brother Mark?"

"Yeah, I killed him. Is that what you want to hear?"

Myles' chin trembled. His arms were shaking. "Get. Out."

"Myles, is that you?" Mrs. Lehman called from the couch. Tanner glanced and saw her stretching from her sleep.

"If you say yes and don't come back, you'll upset her more," Tanner kept his voice low.

Fury building inside Myles. His eyes lit up with anger, boosted by whatever drug he fed his body.

Myles stared right at him. "I'm here, Momma."

"Oh, good. You have a good time?"

Myles cracked his knuckles. "Yep."

"I'll make you breakfast," Mrs. Lehman said, moving out of her chair. Tanner could hear the creak of the recliner going down for her to put her feet down.

"No, Momma. I don't need food." Then he mouthed. "Get. Out."

Tanner shook his head.

Myles jumped toward him, grabbing him by the shirt and shoving him against the corner of the stove. Tanner slid his arms between Myles' and knocked the younger man's hold from him. When Myles went to make a swing, Tanner leaned to his left.

"Stop it!" Mrs. Lehman yelled. "There is no fighting in this house."

Myles ignored his mother's command. He caught Tanner in the jaw, clipping him enough to rattle his teeth. Tanner grabbed Myles and slammed him against the wall near the door. "Cool it! Your mother said, 'stop.'"

Mrs. Lehman fretted inside the doorway. "That's enough."

She went over to the refrigerator, grabbed a yardstick, and Myles visibly flinched.

Mrs. Lehman waved it at them.

Myles struggled against him, but Tanner slammed him back into the wall. "You want a shot at me. We'll take it outside."

Myles brought up his knee. Tanner barely had time to dodge the low blow as the kitchen door opened.

Mariah appeared, her face red and flushed from running. "What is going on here?"

Momma prowled behind the kitchen table. Her yardstick held up, ready to strike.

Mariah's eyes grew large as she took in the scene.

Myles growled and shoved Tanner away.

Tanner backed off, holding up his hands.

"He started it!" Myles marched over to his duffel bag, grabbed it, and headed for the door. "He has no business in this house!"

Myles shoved past her and pushed her back out on the porch as he stalked away.

"Come back here! What's that supposed to mean?"

Tanner kept an eye on Mrs. Lehman. "It's okay, Mrs. Lehman. No fighting. Mariah's home." But the older woman appeared caged and restless.

Her gaze darted from him to the door. Her knuckles are white on the yardstick.

"Mariah?" He moved closer to the door and slipped out to make sure Myles didn't try to throw a punch at his sister, too. She stood with her hands on her hips. "Where are you going now? I need to talk to you. A man was here last evening."

That grabbed his attention for a moment. "What guy?"

"Tattoo on his neck. Scruffy. Said he'd be back to collect. What trouble have you gotten into, Myles?"

"I warned you to stay away from the cabin, but no, you went putting your nose in someone else's business. Just had to go clean the place up, didn't you? Holt isn't anyone you want to mess with, Mariah. You owe him. He collects. Calling the cops won't fix this. I'm out of here."

"He threatened Momma," Mariah said.

"Good."

"You don't mean that."

Tanner put his hand on her shoulder.

Myles tossed his stuff in the back of his truck.

"Where are you going?" Mariah asked. "We need to talk about this."

Myles ignored her, got in his truck, and pulled away.

Mariah moved to go after her brother, but Tanner squeezed her shoulder. "Your mom's upset. You should probably calm her down first."

"Of course." Mariah sighed, turned, and went into the house. "Momma. Are you okay?"

Tanner took his truck keys and headed to the barn to help Pap and Tyler finish cleaning up after milking the cows. Rattled by Myles' assault, he needed to put some distance between them.

He cleaned the pens inside the barn a few days ago. After that, it wouldn't hurt to tackle them again. Temperatures had dropped lower at night, so he ensured the young cattle had a clean and dry place to lie down. Once he finished, Tanner's muscles ached and burned with the pitchfork and shovel workout.

Tyler left for work. Pap rode along to pick up his truck from the tire shop. Someone had sliced all four tires in the woods the day they found the cow shot.

He went into the milk house and grabbed a bottle of water from the little storage area where they kept supplies and the compressor. Myles' angry face, Mrs. Lehman's panicked one, and Mariah's dismay followed him throughout the day.

He had to put a stop to it.

Not everyone can be saved.

"I couldn't save you," Tanner tossed the empty water bottle in a trash can beside the milk house door.

She loves you. You know that, right?

"Go away," Tanner pulled his hat down lower on his head and grabbed his gloves when he saw Mariah riding down the dirt lane toward the barn.

And miss out on all the fun?

Tanner shook his head. Why couldn't he let Mark's memory rest?

Maybe it's not me. It's you.

Tanner chuckled. Just like Mark to use a terrible breakup line.

He went outside to meet Mariah. She dismounted Juniper, holding the reins and staying close to her horse. Mariah changed out of her nursing scrubs and wore a pair of jeans with her boots. She had a warm jacket and a fleece band around her head to cover her ears.

"Your mom, okay?" he asked, surprised she would let her alone this soon.

"Your Pap is at the house. He talked Momma into playing cards with him." Her facial expression twisted. "I saw what happened to the truck. He told me about the other cow. I'm glad you found it, but I wish you would have told me."

"A lot has been happening."

Juniper lowered his head. Mariah ran her fingers through his forelock. "I've never admitted to anyone in my life, but I'm scared. That guy, Holt, asked me for cash and narcotics. I would have lost my job tonight if you didn't let me borrow Tyler's truck. I almost think God didn't want me to go to work. If I lost my job, I couldn't get the narcotics." She leaned into Juniper.

Tanner envied the old horse. He wanted her to lean on him. "We need to call the cops."

"No. Holt said no cops. I can't risk anything happening to Momma." Her face bunched, and Tanner closed his hand over one of hers.

"He threatened you, Mariah."

She took an unsteady breath. "Which is why I called and left a message for the social worker, and I'm going to make arrangements and put Momma in a home. She'll be safer there with around-the-clock care than here." Tears welled in her eyes. "I can't do this anymore, Tanner. They called for pain medications for a patient in my care, and all I could think of was the man's threats."

"Mariah." Tanner ran his hand up her arm.

"I've never seen Myles like this. You and him fighting upset, Momma. Why would you fight with him?"

"He threw the first punch. I was trying to keep it from going further when you came."

Her bottom lip trembled.

"Mariah, it's okay. You can cry. I won't tell anyone." Then Tanner pulled her in closer. Stubborn Mariah, she dashed the tears sliding down from her eyes with her fist.

"Ever the gentleman," she tried to laugh.

"Only with you." He reached up and brushed away a tear. "We'll get through this. Together. I promise."

"No. I don't want your promises. I want my family together. Safe. I came to tell you to stay away. You've caused enough trouble in my family."

"You don't mean this." Tanner tried to draw her toward him. She pulled back.

He held onto Juniper's reins. "What will you do?"

Mariah turned to put her foot back in the stirrup. Tanner's lungs pressed down, suppressing his air.

"I don't know." She swung up in the saddle.

Looking down at him, she said, "I've got three days to figure it out."

"Mariah, if you don't call the police, I will. These guys mean business. If you give him what he wants, he'll return for more because he knows he can intimidate you and get what he wants. This won't help Myles or keep your mother safe. They threatened me, too. Shooting one of our cows was just a warning. Vandalizing Pap's truck is nothing compared to what guys like this Holt will do to get a hold of what they want."

She sucked in her breath and sniffled. He resisted reaching up and pulling her off that saddle to shake some sense into her.

"Madison Peters will be coming over and staying with Momma for the next few nights. See you around."

She reined Juniper to turn. Shocked, he allowed the reins to pull from his hand. She put her heels into the horse and took off in a trot, then a gallop.

See him around?

Was she blowing him off?

Just like that?

What just happened?

17

Tanner went through all the motions of gathering the cows and separating the dry cows from the milking ones.

Inside the milk house, Pap moved the pipes and checked the settings on the compressor. "Figured you would be in a hurry again this evening."

"Mariah has Madison Peters coming over. She doesn't need me anymore."

"Good. I worried the girl wouldn't listen. She has a hard head like her mother sometimes."

"You set Mariah up with Madison Peters."

"Milly asked us to pray for her granddaughter last week at church. Asked for Madison to find a job, something in the evenings to keep her out of trouble. It will be good for the girl to sit with Penny at night. Helps two families."

It might put a young teenage girl in danger, but Tanner restrained from sharing that thought out loud.

His grandfather had tried to help. Molly Peters had been one of his grandma's good friends, just as Penny had been.

He couldn't begrudge his grandfather, trying to do the right thing for both families.

His grandfather had gone to the hospital that night, stayed

with him, and listened as Tanner admitted what had happened.

Most guardians would have screamed and shouted at their teenage wards. His grandfather had patted his arm and stood behind him the entire time. Even when he went to court and they sentenced him to a decade behind bars for manslaughter, his grandfather stayed the pillar of strength in his older brother's absence.

He'd been scared. Terrified. It froze his entire world. Back then, he worried more about what would happen to Pap, Tyler, and Mariah than he worried about what they would do to him.

That same worry he saw etched on Mariah's face earlier.

"We almost ready?" Tyler ducked his head into the milk house. "Pete is waiting for us to come over and help finish that wagon."

"You have chores here on the farm," Pap said.

"Nothing that can't wait. Can I borrow your truck when we get done?" Tanner asked.

"What for?" Tyler asked.

"Mariah's car wouldn't start. So she'll need a ride to work."

Pap interjected, "Tyler can give her a ride."

"I think Tanner wanted to be the one to give her a ride." Tyler winked.

"You need to stay away from that girl. We got enough troubles from that side of the fence, and I can't afford to keep fixing my truck," Pap said.

"I'll build you a new truck," Tanner said.

Pap looked at him skeptically. "Not if you get yourself in another pickle and end up gone even longer this time."

"He's got a point, Tanner. The next time it won't be Pap's truck or even one cow. They come after."

"Then we'll have to go after them. We've got three days

before trouble comes knocking again, and this time someone will get hurt."

"Let the police handle it, bro," Tyler pulled out his keys. "You take Mariah to work. I guess we'll be fixing a car tonight instead of Pete's wagon."

"Thanks," Tanner took the keys.

"Let's get those cows milked."

Once the last group of cows had gone through the parlor, Tanner headed out to catch Mariah and give her a ride.

Pap stepped outside the barn with him. "Tanner, you're just like your father. You've got a big heart, son, but you don't take the time to consider the consequences. I let you run loose, trying to give you time, thinking it best after your mother ran off. You're a man, and you got to take responsibility. Those folks over there, I know you feel bad, but Penny and her girl aren't your responsibility."

"So, we're not supposed to love our neighbor?" Tanner challenged.

Pap wiped his hand with a paper towel. "Tyler thinks you've fallen in love with the girl. That, right?"

He never lied to his grandfather. "And if I have feelings for her?"

"I just want you to make sure they are the right kind and not the ones formed out of obligation or guilt."

"It's not guilt."

"As long as you're sure." Pap scrunched up the paper towel. "Be careful."

Getting in the truck and driving over to Mariah's, Tanner had to ask himself if it was out of obligation. Pulling into the Lehman's yard, he glanced over to the empty passenger side.

Time to move on, Evans.

He got out and noticed the little sedan parked closer to the house. Good, Madison had arrived.

He knocked on the door, and Mariah opened it. "Tanner?

What are you doing here? I told you Madison is staying with Momma."

"Unless you're planning on riding your horse to work, I figured you'd need a ride again."

"Oh," She chewed on her bottom lip. By the dark circles under her eyes, she had gotten little rest. "It's been a crazy day. I forgot about my car. Let me check on Madison, and I can drop you off at the farm on my way."

"I'm not giving you the truck this time, Mariah. I'll take you to work. Then I'll be back to see what I can do to fix your car."

"You don't have to do that. I can find another way."

"If you could have, you would have. So why can't you stop being stubborn and let me help you?"

Mariah glared at him.

And Tanner crossed his arms. "We both know you can't afford to lose your job."

Yeah, he got her there. And she knew it.

She relented. "Okay, just this once. Let me tell Madison I'm leaving."

Several moments later, Tanner held the door open for Mariah. She slid in and closed the door. They drove in silence. He wanted to reach over and hold her hand the whole way there. He tried to reassure her he would always be here when she needed someone. He wouldn't leave her. But he couldn't make that promise.

By the determined look on her face, she wouldn't listen to him, anyway. He pulled up in front of the main entrance to the hospital and barely had the truck in PARK before she opened the door and hopped out.

She had that look where her eyes spoke a thousand words beyond what she said. "Thank you."

"I'll be here in the morning for you."

"I can catch a ride with someone." She meant to keep him away.

"You have my number."

He waited and watched her go inside the building. The passenger seat was empty and quiet on his ride back to the Lehman's.

"You're going to have to find an alternator and two new tires. The back ones are punctured." Tyler walked around Mariah's car as Tanner returned to Mariah's place.

"How'd you get over here?"

Tyler put down the hood of the car. "I walked. Pap was finishing up washing the parlor down as I left. I figured you could use a hand. I called Pete. He's on his way over."

"You sure the tires are punctured." It made little sense. Who would damage Mariah's tires?

Holt wanted money and drugs from her. She needed to get to the hospital.

"Stabbed them tire walls with a screwdriver."

"A screwdriver? How do you figure?" Tanner asked.

Tyler pointed down by the tire. "It's lying there. I wanted to check out the rest of the car to see if anything else was sabotaged before calling the police."

"Find anything?" Tanner walked around Mariah's little sedan. He'd always taken her for a four-wheel-drive kind of girl.

"Just the bad alternator. I went inside and got the keys from Madison. I spooked her when I got here, but then I explained. She's got her laptop open and working on some project for school."

"What about Mrs. Lehman?" Maybe leaving a teenage girl to say overnight with the older woman wasn't a good idea.

Tyler shrugged. "I heard the television on."

"So, it's the alternator?" Tanner ran his hand down his face in anticipation of the job ahead.

"Harvey Daniels might fix the tires. Once Pete gets here, we can take them off and drop them off at his place."

"Mariah will need a new alternator." Unfortunately, he might not get that until tomorrow. Most places closed at nine, and he'd have to run to Shelbyville if the auto parts store in town didn't have one in stock.

"Luke Myers might have a used one at his place. His dad used to work on cars to help folks. There are a few old sedans up in that equipment graveyard at his place."

Luke owned a farm on the other side of town. His father salvaged old farm equipment and pieced them out for parts for those who couldn't find or afford new parts for their equipment. Luke had once been a pro baseball player and had come home to take over the family farm.

It seemed no matter what caused a man to leave, God always had a way of bringing him back to where he belonged.

"I can go there after we get these tires off."

"It'll be fun fishing for an alternator in the dark," Tyler headed to his truck, where he kept tools behind the truck seat.

"If he has one."

Tanner and Tyler had the first wheel of the car off by the time Pete arrived. He'd brought his oldest son, Joel, who wasn't over eight or nine. The little man went straight for the tools, eager to help loosen the lug nuts on the last wheel.

"Call Luke first. He and Bridget were headed to the diner when I picked Anne up from closing up the beauty salon," Pete said.

Tanner tried calling Luke but got no answer.

He left him a message. They'd finished taking off the last wheel, the pole light from the barn, and Pete's truck supplying enough light for three grown men to see what they were doing.

"Do you see that?" Joel stood and pointed beyond the house in the woods.

White plumes of smoke stood out starkly against the night.

"That's no chimney fire," Pete said.

Tyler wiped his hands on his pants. "It's coming from the direction of the hunting cabin."

In the shadows of the light, Tanner could see Tyler's worried expression.

"I'll go check it out." No one had been back at the cabin since the police had last been there. It was a Thursday evening. There were other properties on the other side of the woods. Mariah's brother Matt lived on the other side of the ridge. Either way, someone needed to check it out.

"Not alone," Tyler said.

"I'll go," Joel raised his little hand. "Caden Trout once went on a night hike and said it was cool!"

"This isn't a hike, sport," Pete said. "I'll call the fire department and report the smoke. Joel and I will take the tires. Then I had best take him home. It's a school night."

"Dad!"

"Call me when you know what is going on, and be careful." Pete took his son by the shoulders and directed the child back toward his truck.

"It'll be quicker if we drive," Tyler said, his hand out for his keys.

Tanner fished them out of his pocket, slapped them in Tyler's hand, and raced around the passenger side to get in. One of these days, he'd have enough money saved to get a vehicle of his own.

"It's probably the house over the ridge, it's getting cold out at night, and they probably started up their outdoor wood stove."

"With smoke like that?" Tanner said.

"You never know."

And they didn't know, not until Tyler drove them down the lane and back out the dirt road headed back toward their farm. Across the lane, the gate was locked.

Tanner got out and fumbled with the lock he put there,

trying to stay out of his shadows to dislodge the chain and push it open.

Tyler drove through, and Tanner got back in. As they approached, the sounds of crackling wood and billowing smoke greeted them.

The door to the cabin hung wide open, and smoke filtered out. "I'll call in the fire."

Tanner got out of the truck. Rushing toward the cabin, he covered his face with the end of his shirt. He grabbed his phone, switching on the flashlight app.

"Anyone in here?"

No answer greeted him.

Tyler shouted, "The fire department is on its way."

Tanner called one more time. "Can anyone hear me?"

"I can hear you. Most likely, they set it on fire and took off."

Tyler grabbed a blanket from inside his truck. He left it parked a ways back, off the lane, for the fire engine to come up as close to the cabin as possible. It wouldn't make it. This place was private and used by a few.

Tanner kept his mouth covered. Glowing sparks shot out of the fireplace, and fire crept up the side of the wall where a bookcase fed the flames.

Tyler tried to beat down the flame and smother it. Tanner searched for the fire extinguisher in the kitchen area. They'd taken it. The place on the wall where it should have been was empty.

"Come on. We'll have to wait for the fire department."

Tanner followed Tyler out, coughing as he sucked in the fresh air. By the time the fire department arrived, the cabin would have burned to the ground.

They stayed back by the truck, waiting and watching.

"I should call Matt. He should know what's going on."

"You haven't talked to him in forever."

"It's his cabin, too. You should call Mariah."

"Call and tell her what? That I'm standing here watching the cabin burn? I can see that going well." He called her anyway, not surprised to have to leave her a message.

Twenty minutes later, sirens sounded in the distance. The inside of the cabin was consumed by the fire, and no outside water source to soak any of the trees surrounding it or try to put it out.

Tanner's shoulder blades tightened. He couldn't hear much over the sounds of the sirens coming closer.

"I'll point them in the direction to get up here so they don't pass the road." Tyler headed down the lane.

"It probably would be best if I'm not here when Matt shows," Tanner said.

"He'll have to deal with it."

Tanner wasn't sure Matt was the one who would have to deal. Matt, like Mark, had been like another brother to him. He couldn't avoid looking into the man's face and seeing the rage and disappointment there as he'd seen on other occasions. The last time Tanner had killed Matt's brother. No matter that he'd lost a best friend, Tanner lost more—he'd lost the second family he loved.

Maybe Mariah had been right to push him away. They'd never forgive him.

He headed through the trees, taking the quickest route back to the safety of the farm. The red lights flashed through the trees with the fire engine gunning it up to the cabin.

Movement caught his eye in the flashing. Someone stumbled and waved their arms.

Mrs. Lehman?

18

"Mariah!" Mrs. Lehman groped in the dark. She carried a bucket, half sloshing with water.

"Mrs. Lehman, it's Tanner. What are you doing out here?"

He rushed to get to her side. She jumped back from him in the dark. "Who are you?"

"Tanner Evans. You know me. I'm Silas' grandson. My brother Tyler and I come over to hang out."

She gripped his arm. She'd come out without a jacket, wearing only her housecoat and rubber boots.

"What have you boys done?" Her accusation chilled him to the bone. Not far, men shouted, and the wind picked up. Tiny flakes of snow floated in the air.

Tanner took off his jacket. "You're going to freeze out here without a jacket. Come on, Mrs. Lehman. I'll take you home."

Mrs. Lehman wouldn't budge. Instead, she gripped the bucket handle and tightened her hold on him. "Not until I know my children are safe. Where are they? We have to get this fire out!"

Her voice rose an octave with each word. Her arms trembling.

"Matt's on his way. Mariah's at the hospital. She works there, remember? So your children are safe." He prayed for her to hear the truth in his words and a moment of sanity to return.

"Where are they?" Mrs. Lehman trembled again. "Myles? Where is Myles? And Mark? Don't you try to cover up for them!"

She became more agitated. Letting go of him, she dropped the bucket of water. It fell and spilled at their feet.

"You boys are in a lot of trouble. If Silas doesn't tan your hide, Robert will."

And his father, too, in heaven, he imagined. He stepped in front of her, not wanting her to go any closer to the fire. The firefighter had a hose out, the spritz of water carried in the wind coming shy of where they stood.

"I don't know where Myles is, and Mark is gone. He has been gone a long time."

She stood still, flashes of her warring emotions in the shadows of the dying flames as the firefighters fought to put them out. She sniffled. "Somebody's gonna get hurt."

Tears flooded her eyes. "Help. We have to get help."

She grabbed him and pulled him almost down with force. "Help, please."

"It's okay, Mrs. Lehman. The firefighters will put this out. Your children are safe. Let me take you home. Where is Madison? She's supposed to be taking care of you."

He led her a few steps when she shook her head violently, "I don't know any, Madison."

"The girl that is with you tonight. Madison. Is she at the house? Did you leave her at the house?"

Mrs. Lehman let out a strangled cry. "She was waiting for Myles. That awful man came."

"What, man? Where did he go?"

She shoved hard against Tanner. "Stay away from me!"

Mrs. Lehman tripped as she tried to back away and fell.

As Tanner reached for her, he spotted the blood running down her face. He reached into his back pocket, pulling out one of the paper towels he stuffed while milking cows.

She shied away, her eyes big like an owl. "It's me, Tanner. I'm not going to hurt you. I'm going to help you."

She crawled away from him. Her back was against a tree. "Don't you touch me."

He shouted. "Help. I need help here!"

Unable to leave her, afraid she might wander or hurt herself more, he texted Tyler. He went a little way from her and yelled again.

"Tanner!"

"Over here!"

"What's wrong?" Tyler came.

"I found Mrs. Lehman. She's hurt and scared."

Tyler took off, and two men came back with him. They wrapped Mrs. Lehman in a blanket, and two trained firefighters assisted her until an ambulance arrived.

Sheriff Brady came with them and several officers. "What is she doing out here?"

"I think someone did this, which means you need to send someone to check on Madison Peters at the Lehman house. She was watching Mrs. Lehman while Mariah is at work."

"She could have given Madison the slip," Tyler said.

The alarms would have gone off. Besides, Mrs. Lehman had a routine at night, and someone had done this. Tanner could guess that the dangerous man had been the one to visit Mariah.

"Everything was fine an hour ago when we spotted the smoke," Tyler told Sheriff Brady.

"You were at the Lehman place?" Sheriff Brady asked.

"It was a distraction," Tanner shook his head, trying to clear it. "A guy came to the house the other day. He threatened Mariah. He wanted drugs and cash to replace the ones taken from the cabin."

"Why didn't you call this in?" Sheriff Brady asked.

"I told Mariah if she didn't, I would. I guess I figured she would."

"You know what he looked like?" Sheriff Brady asked.

"Tattoo on his neck, not much taller than Mariah, shorter than me. Couldn't see his hair. He had it covered with a hood. Drove an SUV, dark red."

"Like the one you reported earlier?" Sheriff Brady asked.

"I think I saw him last week at the feed mill. He was waiting around for Myles. He had a truck with a four-wheeler on the bed."

"You should have reported it."

"They weren't doing anything illegal."

"I found a pack of pills in the back of the truck with the feed," Tyler said.

"We established they belonged to Mrs. Lehman. Mariah identified them."

"How did you find them in the truck?"

"Myles helped load the feed that day."

"And Myles had them?"

"You'll have to ask him. I don't know where he is, neither does Mariah."

Mrs. Lehman cried and screamed as the two firefighters tried to look at the injury on her head.

"Tell me about tonight," Sheriff Brady said.

"I gave Mariah a ride to work, and Pete Fisher came over to help us fix Mariah's car. But, unfortunately, someone punctured two of the tires," Tanner said.

There was still something off about all this. There wasn't enough room for the ambulance to come the whole way up to the cabin. They brought a stretcher and took Mrs. Lehman down to the vehicle. All the strangers and the lights, and the commotion had upset her.

"Jessica Lehman is on her way to meet the ambulance at the hospital," a firefighter came and told the sheriff.

"Madison could be out looking for Mrs. Lehman or worse—she could be hurt, too," Tanner said.

"I'll send one of my guys," Sheriff Brady motioned for one officer nearest him to come over. He instructed him to check on the girl at the Lehman's house.

"I should go, too." There was no more he could do here.

They brought the cabin fire under control, and in the morning, they'd all see the charred remains. But, one more thing, Tanner was sure he would get blamed.

"You should go with Mrs. Lehman. You've been watching her at night, and she knows you. It will help keep her calm."

Surprised by his brother's suggestion, Tanner agreed. Mrs. Lehman had panicked and said some out-of-place things right before she fell.

It burned him up inside that someone had done this to her. Guys like Holt, desperate for their next hit or taking a loss on his stash, were the worst kind of dangerous.

He hoped Madison was okay. Although Mariah just lost her babysitter.

"She needs you. Go," Tyler said. "Get in that ambulance. I'll come by the hospital after everything gets settled here."

Sheriff Brady called down to the ambulance and ensured they waited for Tanner.

He held Mrs. Lehman's cold, frail hand. "I'm sorry this happened. I should have been watching out better."

Mariah pulled off her surgical gloves, tossed them in the trash, and headed to the nurses' station. "Did Dr. Harrison sign off on those release papers for room six yet?"

"I'll have them in a minute." Trudy, one of the part-time nurses, slid over the file. "I'm almost finished entering the insurance information for room ten."

Gail raised a brow. She tilted her head, and Mariah moved

closer to where Gail sat down from Trudy. "Computer is slow tonight. How are things at home?"

"I might need a ride after my shift. I let Tanner bring me, but I can't keep letting him do that."

"He can't be all that bad. He painted the barn, sits with your mother, and gives you a ride to get to work."

"If you only knew."

Gail handed her the printout of the release papers. "Dr. Harrison is in room three. You can catch him and get him to sign off. Then you'll be able to move on to the patient in seven." Gail went over to Trudy. "I've got this. Why don't you check on the guy in eleven."

Mariah got Dr. Harrison to sign off with a few jabs at her job performance.

She finished handing the woman instructions and watched as she hobbled out with her husband. She'd kept her mask up as people had been coming in all night complaining of stomachaches and deep-seated colds. The last thing she needed was to catch some nasty virus.

There would be no one to take care of Momma, and Dr. Harrison made it clear dead or alive, Mariah couldn't miss another shift and keep her job.

"Mariah, you've got a call on line two," Gail said.

Instantly her hand went for her phone. Madison had her number.

"Dr. Harrison is in room three. You better take that before he comes out."

Mariah checked her phone. One missed call. Tanner.

Was he calling to tell her something about her car? *Please don't let him have sent Madison home and try to prove she needed him.*

She needed him way too much lately. She couldn't keep relying on him. Mariah couldn't think of him without stirring up those old feelings, reliving that kiss by the barn.

She just needed to stay busy by focusing on her patients, helping them, keeping centered on her job, and not how her heart betrayed her when Tanner came around.

And why had he come around?

Because he found her mother? Because of the guilt of what he did to her brother?

Not at all that he had genuine feelings for her. Not like she had for him. For. So. Long.

It was easier for her to stay centered in the life she made after he disrupted her world. How could he expect her to forgive him when she saw he hadn't forgiven himself? And when he did, he wouldn't come around anymore.

She couldn't handle that or take it, not knowing what would happen after her shift ended. Holt would return.

And she'd made a plan.

"You gonna stand there all night or be useful?" Too late, Dr. Harrison stood before her, holding out a patient's chart. "I need you to go up to the pharmacy, grab these orders, and bring them back down. It seems everyone is having trouble doing anything promptly around her tonight."

Her pulse quickened, and she headed toward the elevator when Gail rushed beside her. "Don't forget your call."

"Take a message. It's probably Tanner, and I can't talk to him right now. I've got to get to the pharmacy and see what's taking them so long for Harrison's med order."

Gail made a face. "Okay, but if he asks me out on a date, remember you're the one who told me to take the call."

Mariah snorted. "Explain that to your husband."

Gail shook her head. "You can explain it when I take you home after your shift."

"Deal."

Mariah hurried to the elevator. Her stomach dropped as the elevator went up. Her phone vibrated in her pocket, and she ignored it.

Taking deep breaths, Mariah put on a big smile as the elevator doors opened. She marched her way down the hall to the hospital's pharmacy. Several people gave her long stares as she passed. Mariah's hands grew slick, holding the med order.

Inside the pharmacy, she handed over the paper and waited. She resisted the urge to check the phone. It could be Madison about Momma.

She swallowed hard, not wanting any distractions from her task.

When the pharmacist handed her the order, she thanked him and returned to the elevator.

Just as the doors were about to shut, three nurses pushed a bed inside with a young man.

Mariah stepped back, holding the tray of painkillers and two small syringes. Her heart beat a little faster with each elevator level taking her back to the emergency room. The bed rolled out on the second floor, and Mariah waited until it closed again. She took hold of the syringe.

She glanced up at the camera in the elevator, rearranging the medication on the tray. She couldn't do this. The last thing she wanted was to go to prison or lose her nursing license.

Shaking in her knees, Mariah stepped off the elevator.

What other choice did she have?

"Mariah, it was Sheriff Brady on the phone," Gail took the tray from her. Otherwise, she might have dropped it.

"There's been a fire at the cabin. Your momma's on her way in by ambulance."

Then she heard her name called over the hospital's intercom system.

19

Tanner stood in the waiting area. He wasn't family, so they hadn't allowed him in.

Behind the doors, they'd paged Mariah, and as soon as she'd come out, her eldest brother Matt went through the emergency room doors.

Myles had been in the waiting room before either of them. He sat with his head in his hands, rocking back and forth in a chair by the magazine rack.

Tanner gave him a nudge, and Myles looked up, spotted his older brother, and shot to his feet. He rushed over to Matt, the younger version of their father, as Tanner remembered him.

For a moment, Tanner thought he'd seen Mark, but Matt had an inch or two of height on the other sibling, and his eyes a different shade of blue after their mother.

Behind Matt, a curvy brunette with a toddler on her hip followed. The child clutched a pink crocheted blanket and a worn stuffed cow.

Matt glowered at Myles. He did not heed Tanner as they went to security and disappeared inside the emergency room.

The woman sat, speaking low to the child. She wrapped the blanket tighter and looked over at Tanner.

"You the one who found Momma Lehman?"

"Tanner Evans."

She looked familiar. Back from high school?

"Jessica Lehman. I think I was a few years ahead of you in school. I graduated with Matt. You're the one who——" She stopped and rethought her words. "Thank you for being there."

"Anytime." He sat close to her, a set of hazel eyes peering at him from beneath the blanket. Her hair was tousled, and her thumb was in her mouth.

"No, don't you do that. You know your daddy doesn't like it," Jessica tried to pull the thumb away. The toddler whined.

She glanced back at Tanner, "Is she okay?"

"I found her out in the woods near the cabin. It looked like she hit her head." Or someone had hit her. He didn't want to place that kind of worry on Matt's wife.

"Matt was right to want to sell that place. It brings nothing but grief."

He made no comment and stared ahead at the doors.

Soon Mariah came out. "She's in room eighteen. They'll be taking her up to a standard room for the night. I'll be up as soon as my shift ends. They'll ax me if I cut early again."

Jessica rose with the toddler in her arms. "I should go meet Matt up there."

"Fifth floor. The nurses will let you know when they have her settled."

She blamed herself. He read it on her face.

Tanner squeezed her arm, trying to reel her in for a hug. But she wouldn't let him.

"I have to go. I'll see you up there," Mariah said, a question more than a statement.

"I'll be waiting right here."

Jessica watched without a word. Mariah's sister-in-law

waited until she returned behind the doors of the ER before stepping in front of Tanner.

Whatever she had to say to him fell silent when Matt and Myles came out.

"They're calling in a social worker."

"So, what does that mean?" Jessica asked.

Myles stood, Matt, listening. His face went as pale as Mrs. Lehman's when Tanner found her close to the cabin.

"We'll finally get her in a home, and she'll have the around-the-clock care she needs," Matt said.

"You should talk to Mariah first," Tanner said.

"This isn't your business, Evans. What are you even doing here?" Matt asked.

"He's the one who found her," Jessica said.

Matt glanced at Myles. "I thought you said you found her?"

"Or is he the reason she was out there this late?"

"Why were you out there this late?" Myles asked defiance in his voice.

"Fixing Mariah's car and ensuring she had a way to work."

"Or setting my dad's cabin on fire," Myles said.

"You have anything to do with that, Evans?" Matt asked.

"Tyler was with me. Don't believe me. Ask him. We're the ones who called it into the fire department."

Myles snorted.

Matt gave him a look that made him sulk back.

"I could say the same about you."

"I have a job. We had a truck come in late. We can't leave until they're all loaded for the morning."

Tanner crossed his arms. "And you parked your truck by the barn and rode Mariah's horse up to the cabin. Only your mother caught you and followed you. "

Myles' eyes narrowed. "You don't know what you're talking about."

"Ask Madison Peters. You sent her home, didn't you? An officer found her at home. She said you told her to leave."

"How do you know?" Matt asked.

"Tyler was with the Sheriff. She also identified Myles' friend. He threatened Mariah the other day. I think you said his name is Holt?"

"Someone threatened, Mariah? And you didn't tell me?" Matt said to Myles.

Jessica's eyes widened.

"You have no business coming around our property Evans." But Myles said, "I warned Mariah. She never listens."

"Myles," Jessica whispered.

"If I hadn't, your mother could have died out in the woods, and no one would have found her except for Mariah when she went looking after finding her gone in the morning. Or maybe one of Myles' friends hiding their dealings up in the cabin. What else did your friends have stashed at the cabin they didn't want anyone to find?"

"The sheriff told me about the drinking parties up at the cabin. Sure it isn't you, Evans?"

"You set the cabin on fire. Then you waited until we left."

"You've got it all figured out, don't you, Evans?" Myles crossed his arms.

"Your mother's injury wasn't an accident, was it?" Tanner lowered his voice and looked at Myles' pale face. "Was it Holt? Or was it you that hit her?"

Myles went white.

"That's enough, Evans. We didn't have any trouble until you came back. How dare you accuse my brother of hurting our mother or any other of the things going on?"

"I've been up there. It's not drinking or underage kids, Matt. I've seen it, and I think Momma has too, which is why they vandalized the barn. Sometimes at night, someone calls and hangs up. It spooks Momma when no one is on the other end of the line. At first, I thought Myles was doing it to be funny and cruel because he was mad about Tanner being in the house."

"Mariah, what are you doing out here instead of in there with Momma?" Matt asked.

"You're all being too loud; I can hear you on the other side of the doors." Her hands planted on her hips. "Myles, please tell me you didn't hurt Momma?"

The young man looked like he'd barf.

Mariah turned to Matt. "Someone called a social worker."

"I did." Matt said, "She can't go home after this. She can't be alone, and you can't watch her all the time."

"That is why I have already spoken to the social worker and made arrangements to get help with Momma since Myles ditched his duties." Mariah glared at her younger brother.

"He's got a job and school. He can't be babysitting Momma. You can't go tying him down with responsibilities that aren't his," Matt said.

"Oh, and you can? You got him the job, didn't you?" Mariah asked.

"We're all trying to help," Jess said.

Tanner stepped back, not wanting to get involved in their family feud. He stood behind Mariah, staying close enough for her to know he had her back.

"A man needs to learn to make his way," Matt said.

"If you want to sound like Dad, take your own advice, Matt. Because Dad would have said we take care of our own, we take care of each other, and when is the last time you've come over to the farm to visit with Momma? When is the last time you've offered to help?"

"I am trying to take care of Momma. You're the one who keeps screwing everything up!"

Mariah leaned back, her back against Tanner's chest. His hands went up to her arms to let her know he had her.

"Just because you can't stand to live on the farm anymore doesn't mean the rest of us have to lose our home, too. It's the only place Momma wants to be. Daddy built that house for her, for us, and I won't let you take that away."

"You have no choice," Matt balled his fist. "I'm the oldest. Dad left it to me to take care of this family."

"Until you walked away after Mark died and Daddy changed the will," Mariah said, keeping her voice low.

A woman with a young girl crying came into the emergency room's waiting area.

"Momma goes into a home, Mariah. You can't stop the sale of the farm for all of us to get our share. You're being selfish. I've got a family to take care of, and Myles is trying to go to school."

"I'm selfish?" Mariah asked. "Me?"

"Lehman family?" A woman in scrubs and a clipboard stepped out. They all turned to look at her.

"You're the one who brought trouble back to our family," Matt glared at Tanner.

"This isn't the place," Jessica leaned into Matt. "Come on, let's check on Momma Lehman."

Matt nodded. He took the toddler from Jessica's arms, smoothed down the rising hairs of static electricity from the dry air on the child's head, and motioned for Myles to follow.

The entire time, the younger brother stayed quiet, and Tanner whispered to Mariah, "Get one of those urine tests done on your brother."

"I don't think it was Myles."

"We'll let the sheriff handle that, but you can be sure he's not standing there without some kind of buzz. Look at his eyes."

The door behind them opened, "Mariah, we need you at bed six."

"I'll speak with you shortly," the woman in scrubs said, leading Matt, Jessica, and Myles to an office on the other side of the waiting room.

"Myles is coming with me. It'll only take a few moments."

Her younger brother's face contorted, and he glanced at Matt.

"Go on," Jess said. "We're not going anywhere."

And neither was he.

Tanner stared out the window into the darkness. A shine in the black asphalt of the parking lot stretched under the pole lights.

Give me the keys, Mariah.
I want to go, too.
You'll get in trouble.
I don't care.
I'll come back for you.
Then I'm staying right here until you do.
Promise.
I promise.

It took him long enough. Sorry for her brothers. He had a promise to keep.

20

"Your shift is over, Mariah. Why don't you take that handsome cowboy who's been hanging out in the waiting room most of the night for some coffee?"

Mariah hadn't expected him to stay. Gail gave her a look, and Mariah figured she'd better get that coffee or offer, anyway. Gail seemed to relax as she sighed with resignation. "Just one more trouble in my life."

"If that's trouble, then I'd take it," Chloe, one of the new nurses coming on shift, winked at Mariah.

From here, peering through the window slots of the double doors, she saw Tanner staring at the television.

It did something unpleasant to her inside, and it downright hurt to see him still here. He had a shadow creeping up that firm jaw of his, and his hair looked like he'd run his hands through it several times to keep it from hanging over his eyes.

Gail gave her a little push as she walked by. "Go on. If he bites, that's part of the fun."

Mariah felt a blush heat her cheeks.

She hadn't thought about their kiss, but her thoughts turned to his lips. The way he'd kissed her inside the barn always came back to her mind.

He'd been timid and thirsty, sipping at first, then going for the chug, and she'd been right there with him. Would she ever have enough of him?

She pushed him away, and he kept pushing back.

Her life had become complicated. This—him and her—pushed at her emotions.

Could she ever accept him, all of him, and move past the accident that severed him from her in the first place?

They had more to overcome with Myles' drug addiction. Her brother might never forgive her, and she could live with that.

At least Matt had stepped up alongside her while they had given their younger brother a choice. Only Myles could decide what happened next.

Tanner seemed to know she'd been looking at him, his face turned, and those eyes, tired and weary, gazed in her direction.

They pulled her through the double doors. Mariah walked up to him. "Coffee?"

He looked at her, long and hard, and she waited as his eyes drifted down over her plain blue scrubs. When his gaze came back to meet hers, a soft smile crept on his lips. "I figured you'd want to go straight up and see your Mom."

"If that were true, you would have left by now. Come on, it'll be sunup soon, and you'll need to get back to the farm. I'll even drive you so you don't fall asleep."

Those last words sent unease through her. She reached out and took his hand. "The cafeteria is this way."

"You want coffee here?"

"It's not so bad. And I can peek in on Momma before we head out."

"I guess it isn't visiting hours."

"I'm a nurse. I'm sure I can sweet talk the floor nurses to seeing her before I get you home and come back when I can visit. She'll have at least another day."

His fingers entwined with hers, warm and firm, and she squeezed them for comfort. Funny, she wanted to put distance between them less than twenty-four hours ago.

"I'm sorry about what happened earlier," he said as they rode the elevator to the third floor.

"It's not your fault. I'm grateful you were there for Momma." And she meant it.

They grabbed two coffees. Tanner threw in a muffin before he paid.

They found a small round table in the back part of the cafeteria. A few EMTs sat on the other end, probably ended their shift too, or waiting for another call in between runs.

Tanner broke his muffin in half, offered her a piece, and she shook her head. She never could eat right away when she got off work. Working three twelve-hour shifts a week got brutal at times, but it allowed her time home with Momma, especially since Myles hadn't been as mature and understanding with their deal as she had assumed.

It twisted her gut to know Matt had once more tried to take control of their lives and decide what was best. How could he know what was best when he'd hightailed it far away from the farm as soon as he could?

What gave him the right to influence Myles' life and complicate hers?

After tonight, things would change again.

"Hey," Tanner said softly. "It's going to be okay."

She took a sip of her coffee. God had shown up tonight, as he'd shown up weeks ago, and every time Tanner had been there to protect Momma. Even if Momma lay in a hospital bed on another floor, she was alive and safe. Mariah shuddered to think what could have happened if he hadn't.

Myles admitted Holt had put him up to setting the fire at the cabin.

Neither of them had planned on Tanner sticking around to fix her car.

Was this all an attempt for Tanner to make amends for what happened to Mark?

Mariah shook her head. She wouldn't let Matt dictate what was right or wrong. God knew, and she had to trust in that, even if she didn't always agree.

"Momma, maybe. I know that. Maybe Matt is right. I should have given up a long time ago. It seems like I'm the only one fighting to hold on to making this work." She stared down at the lid of her coffee. "I should have known from the start this would never last."

"You're tired. It's been a long night. You'll see things differently in the morning."

"I don't think so." She closed her eyes and squeezed back the pressure of needing to cry. Not here, not with Tanner, not when she tried to end this before it went any further. Too stubborn to give up. Just. Like. Her.

She hadn't gone to see him back then, and it ate at her as much as it pained her on the day she watched them lower her brother's casket to the ground. Her family pretended Tanner no longer existed and buried him in their minds along with Mark. Of all the things her mother forgot over the years, Momma held on to those memories.

"You're the strongest woman I've ever met, Mariah Lehman. Don't you go giving up now," Tanner said.

It brought a sad smile to her lips. Even the strong got tired, and she could feel the ache deep in her bones. Stop fighting it, Mariah. Just let go. She couldn't save Mark. What made her think she'd change things and save her own family by forgiving Tanner and allowing him back in her heart.

She had become as foolish now as she'd been back then.

Her heart belonged to him.

It didn't matter when or how, or why it happened.

It just did.

"You know, every day I come here," she told him. "I see the people sick and hurting and the doctors with the knowledge and the medicines to fix what ails them, and it never ceases to astonish me that no matter how hard you try or how much you ask for or try to beg and bargain, it sometimes isn't enough."

Tanner tilted his head, listening.

"I wanted to be a doctor. I wanted to save people. Dad disagreed that I should go to college, being a girl and all. Myles was too young. Matt took Dad's side. Momma wouldn't say a word, of course, in front of Dad. Thankfully, Mr. Mullens at school helped me fill out the papers, and I got a scholarship. Not enough for University, but I could live at home and drive to nursing school. Dad agreed. I should have listened to my father."

"And done what?"

Mariah shrugged. "I dated Greg Matthews after you left."

"Not Sam Brink?"

Mariah blinked, momentarily stunned by his assumption. "No. Everyone knew Sam had a thing for Caroline Adams."

"Greg still around?"

Did she detect a hint of jealousy? "No. He went to MIT and stayed here. I think Dad thought I'd marry him and settle down with a bunch of kids."

"I'm glad you didn't," Tanner said.

"We were only ever friends."

"Like you and me?"

"Were we?" she asked, "Friends?" She took another sip of her coffee. She must have been more tired than she thought to tell him all this. It made her search deep down how she felt about him. About them.

The truth was, she hadn't been able to keep away from him then, and she'd be lost without him now. She'd survived the years, and whether or not she wanted, she could learn to live without him again.

"Maybe not back then," he admitted, "But I'd like to think we are more than that."

It was the more she wasn't prepared to handle and finished her coffee so they could go. "I'll go check on Momma. Those cows of yours won't wait long if you're to get them milked on time."

Tanner didn't bother looking at his watch. "Tyler and Pap can start without me if need be. They've been covering the mornings without me."

"I don't want to get you in trouble." Mariah got up, grabbed her empty cup, and tossed it in the trash as they headed out. If she didn't, her mouth might loosen more and tell him things only she and God needed to know.

One of the EMTs waved. Mariah waved back out of habit. She headed to the elevator. "I won't be long."

"I'll go up with you. Stay in the hall since I won't be allowed in."

As the elevator doors closed, Tanner turned her toward him. "You wanted to be a doctor?"

She sniffled, getting a grip on herself, pulling back her shoulders, and remembering they were in a hospital. And she was still a nurse, off duty or not.

"Yeah, I did."

"But not now?"

Mariah watched as the elevator counted floors. "All I ever wanted was to be in the emergency room, help people, save lives. Always felt the people here needed me most."

"Because you couldn't save Mark?" Tanner put his arms around her.

Soothing, comforting, making her think once more that it was right to let him close.

"It wasn't your fault." He swallowed, and she watched the motion of his neck muscles tighten, wanting to place a kiss there. "It was mine."

"It was mine, too." She let the tears escape. All these years, she'd carried the knowledge, hated it more than she ever hated Tanner. "I didn't have to give back those keys."

"You can still go be a doctor, Mariah." His head dipped lower.

She held onto his arms, rising on her toes. "And if I don't want to?"

"Then that's okay, too." His forehead touched hers, and his lips brushed across her cheek, the sensation of it sending a ripple of warmth. The elevator came to a stop.

Two nurses and an X-ray technician stepped inside. Mariah stepped out of the elevator in a hurry. "Off duty," she muttered as she headed down the hall.

Stupid Mariah, just stupid.

And so right. She hated the curl of her belly and the regret hovering over her for the interruption.

She checked at the desk, Tanner waiting there for her. She slipped in to find her mother resting in a room around the corner.

They'd turned on the television. A game show played quietly in the background. Mariah brushed a strand of her mother's hair from her face and whispered, "I'm here, Momma. You always told me to do what was right, and I promise I will. I love you."

She kissed her mother's forehead and stepped out of the room.

Her mother aged in there, and the scents of sick and clean made her nauseous.

They never bothered her before.

She took one look at Tanner, knowing they'd have to go back down that elevator together, and dreaded what she had to do.

She waited, waited until they got to the parking lot. Mariah held out her hand for his keys. "I think this should be the other way around, don't you?" he teased.

"I'm driving. You've been up all night."

"So have you."

"I'm used to it." She moved before Tanner could argue or

try to talk her out of it. She knew he could, and he would. He had once before, a long time ago. Inside the truck, she stared at the keys, stared harder when she put them in the ignition, and prayed they'd both get home safe this morning.

Safe.

She'd become her mother.

And she could hear her father after Mark's accident, after Tanner's trial. *"There won't ever be an Evans on Lehman land again, you hear?"*

"I hear you, Daddy, loud and clear."

"What did you say?" Tanner asked, shutting the passenger-side door.

"Buckle up."

21

Mariah hadn't slept in twenty-four hours, forced to take a double shift, and the girls on the floor had given her an empty bed during one of the lunch breaks to catch some sleep. Only Mariah had been afraid one hour would be worse than none.

Myles had gone with the police officers who showed up at the hospital. She suspected he'd gone to stay at a drug rehabilitation center. He'd given the police the description and information they needed to search and arrest Holt. The police had located Holt's buddy Dave and two others in a trap house near the community college in Shelbyville. The guy could have gone anywhere, and Mariah couldn't ask Myles.

They took his phone and restricted outside communications until he completed the rehab program. Until then, she asked God to worry about him for once, lifting the anxiety and burden from her.

Eventually, Holt would show up on her doorstep.

It was past the deadline he'd given her.

Sheriff Brady had assigned an officer to check regularly on the house.

Her brain had shut off after the middle-aged woman blew chunks all over her rubber shoes. Good thing she had never been the squeamish kind. Momma was still in the hospital. She'd sat down with the social worker who came to the hospital to meet with her again.

Matt could voice his opinion, but the only one to decide whether Momma went to Woodcrest was her. *I'm so tired, Lord. I can't do this alone.*

She accused her brother of being the controlling one, and maybe it had been her all along. If she could keep Momma at home, help Myles afford to go to school, and maybe, just maybe, Matt would come back, and they'd be whole again.

Tanner and Tyler fixed her car, and Pete Fisher showed up with her new tires. She had to remember to thank him at church the next time she saw him.

Inside the kitchen, she tossed her keys on the counter and dumped her bag on a chair. The scent of eggs and bacon made her stomach roll. She vaguely remembered a banana from the cafeteria.

A steaming cup of coffee sat on the table, black with cream and sugar beside it.

"I couldn't remember how you liked it." Matt stood by the stove, a spatula in his hand.

He plated scrambled eggs and placed them on the table. "You look dead on your feet."

"What are you doing here?" She crumbled into the nearest chair.

"I brought Momma home. I took the day off and figured you would need some sleep, I can't do this every day, but Jess said she'd bring Brooklyn over and visit to help since she'll be staying home more now that we're expecting again."

"Congratulations." Mariah took the fork Matt slid her way.

He turned a chair, sat on it, and leaned against the back. "I have only ever wanted what was best for this family."

She poked at the eggs waiting for them to cool. None of the men in her family knew how to cook, so this was a first.

"Then why did you bring Momma home? I thought they were waiting for a bed to send her to Woodcrest."

"She kept asking when she could come home. She couldn't remember why she'd been there. I figured here was better for her than in a strange place. I hadn't realized Momma had, well, slipped so much."

"She sleeps most days. It's at night she wanders as her mind does. Myles should have said something to me." Mariah kept pushing around the eggs, exhaustion filling her bones with lead.

"Would you have listened?"

"And you did? You closed yourself away from us, from me, and you'd listen to him and not me."

Matt ducked his head. "I think part of me has always blamed you for what happened to Mark. It leaves a void inside, you know?"

"I know." Then she looked around and asked. "Do you know where he is? Myles?"

"I drove him to Louisville yesterday, and he admitted himself into a rehabilitation center. I think he wanted to avoid dealing with the police. He knows what he did was wrong, and he feels even worse since Momma got hurt."

"Tanner was right."

"Yeah. I was wrong."

It took a lot for her brother to admit that.

"Did he say how Momma got hurt?"

"Holt came in the house after Madison left. Holt was going through the place, wanting cash and drugs. Momma tried to stop him. Myles tried to stop Holt. They got into a fight, and Momma disappeared into the woods. Holt took off when he heard the sirens. Myles was in the woods looking for Momma."

Mariah's entire body got chilled. "Tanner said he found Momma up by the cabin."

"Imagine my shock when Tyler called me. I haven't

spoken to him—in a long time." Matt cuffed the back of his neck. "What was any of the Evanes doing hanging around here?"

"Tanner found Momma one night wandering in the woods. Then we discovered what was happening in the cabin."

"They shot one of their cows. The sheriff showed me the pictures of what they did to our barn. I should have been here. You shouldn't have had to take this all on your own."

"I had Tanner."

"I can't say I'm happy about that, but Myles told me something is going on between you two."

Mariah took her first bite of eggs, something less dangerous than admitting she had feelings for Tanner. The last thing her brother needed to hear was that she'd fallen in love with the boy next door, the one who'd been driving under the influence and responsible for Mark's death.

"It wasn't his fault," she said, reaching for her mug of coffee, needing the caffeine to boost her confidence. "I was there, too. I was the one who'd been driving first."

Matt's brows furrowed. "What are you talking about?"

"Mark said I could go. He said I could be the driver so Dad wouldn't get mad."

"As if," Matt said.

"Yeah, well, Meg and Anne and that Lisa girl Tanner had been making cow eyes at were all going to be there, too."

"Then Mark got plastered and mad and decided we had to go find Angie, but Tanner talked me into giving him the keys, and he'd take Mark since I was supposed to be at Anne's. He promised to come back for me later."

Mariah closed her eyes, trying to push away those last moments of seeing her brother angry and brooding as he did when he'd drank too much. None of them should have been there. None of them had been of age.

I'll come back for you.

I promise.

Mariah gave her head a swift jerk. Not even the caffeine could keep her from drowning in exhaustion.

Matt reached under her and pulled the plate away. "Go to sleep, Zombie. I took yesterday and today off, so I'll be around. We still need to talk about Momma."

"I made arrangements for her to stay at Woodcrest. They are willing to work with me, and Momma will only stay there on the nights I work. I'll take her a few times to visit for her to get used to it."

"If you're sure."

"I know I can't do this alone. It will be good for Momma to be around other people again and not closed up in the memories of this house." She trudged up the stairs, pausing by the recliner chair.

"She's in her room."

Mariah glanced across the living room to the old sunroom that had become her mother's bedroom.

"Mariah."

She paused her hand on the railing.

"Tyler made an offer to buy the cabin."

"It's burnt down." She would handle those emotions later when the shock and the adrenaline had gone down.

"He wants to rebuild it and have a place of his own. I think we should sell it to him. It's a small piece. It would help pay for Momma's care and Myles' college."

Not to mention the cost of the rehab. Her brother was thinking about it, but Matt didn't have to say it out loud.

Pulling herself up the stairs to her room, she could have been one of the walking dead from that television series some of the other nurses talked about in passing.

She would shower later, she decided, going straight into her bed.

Thank you, Jesus, she sighed. Her head settled on the pillow.

Momma had come home, and so had Matt. She'd count her blessings one at a time.

Tyler Evans could have the land. What had been would never be again. It was time for them all to build something new.

22

Snow drifted in the air, small flakes like tiny dust crystallizing in the cold. Juniper's breath came out as streams of white when he snorted at her entering the barn. Things were quiet. Almost too quiet. She took her time, allowing Juniper to eat while she brushed him down. She hummed, no particular tune, as she walked around him and undid the tangles in the gelding's tale.

He munched on hay until she pulled him away. He took the bridle with ease, but she saddled him slowly.

It felt odd, she decided, not needing to rush or worry about getting back to Momma. By the look of exhaustion in Matt's eyes, he needed this time to spend away from things at home. Some downtime with Momma might restore him.

Her brother had always been a hard case to crack. He would run himself to the ground rather than admit he couldn't hold it all together.

Maybe they'd both inherited a little of their father.

She led Juniper outside of the barn. She grabbed gloves and wore a vest over her long sleeves in anticipation of the cold. The trees would shield her from the wind or tunnel the cold breeze directly at them. She hoped for the former.

Riding Juniper, having a chance to breathe—that brought peace to her troubled soul.

The burnt cabin wasn't the only sight she wanted to see. Mariah mounted while Juniper stood like a perfect gentleman waiting for her to get settled.

She gave him the cue to walk, choosing the path through the pasture to the corner gate. It opened to the woods and the small trail to the cabin.

The smell of ash and fire assaulted the scent of dampness and snow.

If it continued to snow like this, they'd have a dusting in a few hours.

She reined Juniper in front of the pile of burnt logs, and the cabin remains. Charred wood, broken glass, and the skeleton of the old couch where the living room was once located opened bare without walls and spilled its contents into the forest.

"No more parties here." She patted Juniper. "Or would Tyler have one once Matt gave him the news?"

No matter. She and Juniper moved on before the gathering mix of emotions stopped her from doing what she intended.

She headed down the lane from the cabin. The gate swung open, and the chain dangled.

She and Juniper took the road, avoiding a few ruts worn from the little traffic they got between the farms.

She heard the hum of the motor of a vehicle coming toward her. She pressed Juniper's side to move him off the road.

A dark red SUV gunned it. The motor got louder, and Mariah could hear the transmission kicking into a higher gear.

It should have slowed down. Mariah's heart did. Juniper pranced as she pulled him back against the slope of the forest.

Mariah glanced behind her. Too steep for Juniper to go back any farther.

The SUV had plenty of room to pass her. She held her

breath and held Juniper steady as the vehicle raced toward them.

It hogged her side of the road. The wrong side.

Quickly, she turned Juniper and urged him into a run. Lifting herself out of the saddle and leaning forward, she glanced over her shoulder. The SUV was gaining on her with no sign of passing.

She darted across the road, pressing her heels harder into Juniper to jump the slight rise from the road to the forest. He hesitated, jumped, and Mariah gripped the saddle horn to stay on.

The SUV blared its horn, Juniper wavered, startled by the blaring noise, and Mariah was a goner.

She flipped forward and to the side, her opposite foot slipping from the stirrup and her grip not enough to hold the force of her weight.

She landed on the hard, cold ground.

The SUV skidded to a halt.

She rolled over. Her bones jarred from the fall. Someone got out of the SUV. She spotted the dark hooded sweatshirt.

"Juniper," she whispered.

The horse spooked, galloping through the trees in the opposite direction of home.

Slowly, Mariah sat up. Nothing was broken except for her pride; she'd have a good bruise on her hip. She reached for a tree to pull herself up when a hand grasped her.

All the blood drained from her face.

"Get up." Holt yanked her up.

Mariah got steady on her feet. Her backside and her hip throbbed from the impact of the fall. Holt's jeans were ripped and stained, his left blue sneakers unlaced.

"You almost killed me."

"I know." Deadly intent glinted in his eyes. He reached behind him, pulling out a handgun. Pointing it at Mariah's head, he said. "That horse of yours would have marked my vehicle. This will only put a mark on you."

Too stunned to say a word, he hauled her toward the SUV. "Get in. Run, and I'll shoot. Reach for your phone, and you're dead."

"Where are we going?" Numbness took over her limbs. She recognized the signs of shock and fear, shutting down her body's reflexes.

"Unfinished business. Get in unless you want me to end it here." He pressed the gun to her head—cold metal bit into her temple.

Mariah got in the SUV.

He pointed the gun at her. Walking around the front of the SUV, Holt got in beside her. The SUV was still running. He gripped the steering wheel with one hand and held the gun with the other. "Put it in Drive."

Biting her lip, she reached over slowly and did as he asked.

When her hands went to her pockets, he said, "Keep your hands out where I can see them."

"What do you want?"

Without answering, he turned them around, cutting a sharp three-point turn, and headed back the way he'd come. "I warned you and that brother of yours what happens when you mess with my business."

His beard had grown longer, his cheeks shallower, and his skin the yellow tone of jaundice.

He jerked the wheel, not slowing, and turned sharply up the lane toward the burnt cabin.

Mariah's mind raced. Juniper ran the wrong way.

How long before Matt got worried that she hadn't returned?

"You should have taken your business elsewhere."

She might as well speak her peace while she had a chance. There was no way Holt would let her live, not with that wild, rage-filled look in his eyes. He slammed on the brakes close to the cabin. "We'll get out here. I don't want extra tracks for the police to follow."

Little spots of snow gathered on the ground. He nudged Mariah out of the vehicle. She stomped her boot into one and left a footprint. As Holt exited the car, Mariah took off, running into the wooded area.

Behind her, Holt swore. He fired his gun, and Mariah covered her head, the bullet embedding in a tree a few yards away. She kept close to the trees, not looking back, and asking God to keep her alive long enough to spill her guts to Tanner on how she felt about him.

Holt swore again. Mariah could hear him moving through the forest after her. First, she went downhill, using the trajectory to give her speed, then her feet couldn't keep up with her.

The slope of the hill brought her down.

Mariah grabbed onto a tree catching herself before she fell. Then, another shot hit the tree she hugged, and she froze.

Catching her breath, she glanced around her. Too much space between the trees, she didn't reach another without Holt's aim finding her.

His colorful language helped monitor his closeness. Mariah pressed against the tree, peering around it as Holt came down the slope, careful of his footing. His gun aimed at where she hid.

"Come out from behind that tree, Nursie," Holt stopped, panting. The gun quivered as he held it in her direction.

"No."

She huddled close, her lungs taking in the cold air and sweat running down her forehead. Her ribs ached along with her hip, but the pain edged her on.

"Have it your way," he said.

Mariah's heart pounded in her chest. Desperate, she looked at her feet; she needed anything to protect her.

Fool, he has a gun.

She shuffled her feet on the ground and picked up a stone at the base of the tree.

Holt came closer, his eyes narrowing on her and the tree. Waiting until he came within her throwing distance, she wailed the rock in his direction. He moved out of the way, and Mariah took off again for the next tree.

Holt's gun went off, the sound echoing in her ears. A hot slice of metal cut into her arm. She slammed against the tree, gripping her arm.

"I said, don't run."

She swallowed down the bile rising in her throat.

Blood seeped through her sleeve between her fingers. She stifled down a sob.

"I can get you the money. You don't have to do this," she pleaded.

"I am afraid I do. Now start walking back up that hill."

Chest heaving, pain radiating through her arm, Mariah marched back up the hill.

"To the cabin."

"You're going to kill me."

"Like I said. No one messes in my business. That farm boy of yours will be next. Too bad he'll be going back to prison."

"You tried to set him up."

It made sense now. He used Myles to get Tanner out of the way.

"The police around here are too slow to ever catch anyone."

"So why don't you just kill me and get it over with?"

Holt pressed the gun to her back and pushed her the rest of the way up the hill. "Oh, I will. First, we have some business to settle."

"I told you I would get you the money."

"I don't want money from you, Nursie. It's too late. You are too much trouble."

They were back at the cabin. Holt shoved Mariah toward the charred remains. "Down on your knees."

He grabbed her injured arm. Mariah screamed from the sudden pain, falling to her knees.

He pressed the gun to the back of her head.

Mariah closed her eyes, holding her breath. *Lord, this was it. Please take care of Momma, and don't let Tanner think this was his fault, too.*

Sounds of a twig snapping made her breath hitch.

"Put the gun down." Tanner's voice rang through the woods.

Holt shoved the gun farther against her head. "Come closer, farm boy, and I'll shoot."

"And I'll shoot you," another voice said from the other side of the cabin. Mariah's gaze lifted. Tyler Evans walked out from between the trees. A hunting rifle pointed toward Holt.

She didn't dare turn her head.

From behind her, she heard the sounds of someone approaching. "It's two against one. You pull that trigger, and you'll be dead before she is."

Mariah honed her gaze on Tyler. He kept Holt in the sights of his rifle scope.

"I didn't take you for the killing kind, farm boy. I don't think you'd do it." Holt cocked his gun. Mariah made a stifled noise as the end of the barrel dug farther into the side of the back of her head.

"I spent ten years in prison for killing a man. But I'd gladly spend a lifetime in prison to protect the woman I love."

Love? Did Tanner say the L-word?

Mariah trembled. Her body shook enough for Holt to notice and grip her shoulder.

Tyler moved closer. "He ain't lying. I'd put down the gun."

Mariah counted her heartbeats. Grateful for each one. Tyler caught her attention.

His frown sent a spark of alarm through her. He tilted his

head, angled to the side, and she didn't hesitate. Over the years, she'd dealt with her share of disorderly patients. She lurched up from her knees so fast. It sent Holt stumbling back a few steps.

Tanner's arms wrapped around them as Mariah turned. She grabbed Holt's hand with the gun, trying to point it away. Tyler rushed forward, "Out of the way."

She moved, and Tyler aimed the gun at Holt's chest. Holt threw his head back, slamming it into Tanner's nose. Blood gushed out, but Tanner didn't release him.

Tyler swore, dropped the gun, and landed his fist across Holt's face. The gun went off, and Mariah's thigh was sliced with pain. She stumbled back, falling to the ground.

Tyler disarmed Holt, and Tanner tossed him to the ground. He grabbed the rifle and said, "Stay down, or I'll kill you."

Tyler took the gun from Tanner. "You see to Mariah. I'll take care of this one."

Tanner bent down by Mariah, his face pinched and his eyes filled with concern. "Tell me what to do, Mariah."

"Pressure. You need to put pressure on it to stop the bleeding." Her head spun, and she felt woozy.

Tanner pressed his hands to her thigh.

"It's going to be okay." He kissed her forehead.

Mariah put her hands over his. "Go call the police. I'm not going anywhere."

Tanner scowled at her. "Tyler called Matt when Juniper came running to our place. We called the police as soon as we saw the SUV. Help is on the way, Mariah. Just stay with me."

She would.

Her head spun faster. Her vision blurred, and she closed her eyes. "Did I hear you say you love me?"

"Yeah, I did." She detected a hint of challenge in his words.

"It took you long enough," she muttered and moaned

when he tilted her head and placed his jacket under it. She opened her eyes and stared into his. Pressing a hand to his cheek, she said, "I have loved you for a long time. I never thought you'd come around to love me back."

He kissed her. Gentle as if she were a piece of glass and would crack with the slightest pressure. She slipped her hand behind his neck and held it so she could kiss him properly. Her lips demanded what her heart had waited for all this time.

Scuffling erupted behind them, and Tanner turned his head away momentarily. "There is a rope on the four-wheeler. Let me grab it, and we'll tie him up until the police arrive."

Tanner gave her another quick kiss. "Be strong. I'm coming back, and we'll get you to a hospital."

23

Mariah woke to the familiar scents of the hospital. A heart rate monitor on her finger and the machine beside her continued to draw its wavy line to show she was alive.

Dear God, she'd survived.

Barely.

It hadn't been a dream, not when a warm hand slid over the one embedded with an IV. Gentle. Firm. Callused fingers meshed between her cold ones.

"Hey."

"Hi." She gazed over at Tanner. Her mouth felt like she'd swallowed cotton or a desert had taken up residence there.

They'd given her good medicine. Strong. The cold drip of it eased into the vein in her hand. She'd be out again soon. Already, she could hardly keep her eyes open.

No pain.

Which was a good sign. Mariah licked her lips and turned her head.

"Let me get you a sip of water."

He poured her some water from the Styrofoam cup on the tray by her bed. Using the controls of the bed and a pillow he picked up from the chair, Tanner helped her sit up.

It smelled dangerously like him.

Had Tanner been sleeping in the chair?

She took a few sips at a time.

"I'll go tell them you are awake. Gail has been coming in every few hours to check on you."

"Tanner," it came as a whisper.

"I'll be right back."

It all happened at once. A delayed response to the danger to her life threatened by living and being alive. Mariah couldn't put words to the congestion in her chest, not pain, more like relief. And she cried. Fat, salty-tasting tears rolled down her cheeks in great gushes.

The cops came, and then, shortly after, the paramedics secured her injuries and got her to the hospital. Tanner had ridden with her.

He came closer, reaching for her and then pulling back. He looked confused and lost through the blur of her tears. Probably because he didn't know what to do, maybe he was afraid he would hurt her. She wasn't sure he wouldn't.

He appeared as he did the night he left her behind all those years ago. It made her cry harder.

"Are you in pain?" he asked.

She shook her head, not able to explain to him. It wasn't a physical pain bothering her so much as an emotional one.

A delayed reaction.

Tanner eased over and retook her hand. With the other, he reached over and pressed the call button by her bed.

"Do you remember what happened?" He asked as if she could have forgotten. But, oh no, she wouldn't let him off the hook that easy. Not this time.

He said he loved her, and God knew she loved him.

She would not let him go this time.

"Mariah?" Those eyes of his could make her insides turn to mush.

"Back away and give the girl room to breathe," Gail's voice boomed from behind Tanner.

He held up his hands and backed away.

Mariah sniffled, trying to get ahold of her emotions.

Gail grabbed tissues and held them to her nose.

Mariah took over the tissues and blew.

"What are you doing here?"

"Are you kidding? You know you could have been killed, right?" Gail pushed Tanner off to the side. "You're lucky that horse of yours has a sense of direction."

"Where is Juniper?" she asked, frowning.

"He's over in the heifer shed at Pap's place. We'll bring him home once you can care for him again."

"Thank you. I figured I'd have to search for him when he ran in the wrong direction. It's not like Juniper to run off or to go in the wrong direction." Her throat was scratchy, and she took another sip of water.

"I think he went where he needed to go," Gail said.

"Are you on shift?" Mariah asked.

"I am. I'll be back again later. Dr. Harrison has been conferring with Dr. Paul, the surgeon, on your care. Said he is doing his duty to ensure you are back to work in as little time off as possible, but we all see he is worried about you."

"I'm going to be off work for a while, aren't I?" Mariah laid back. She couldn't care for her mother when she most likely couldn't walk alone for a while. That bullet to her thigh would slow her down for several weeks.

"Think of it as a vacation. You need to rest," Gail patted her shoulder. "Dr. Paul will be in later to see you. I'll have Cheryl send in some Jell-O. We've got the lime kind today."

"Oh, goodie," Mariah said.

Gail hurried off, not without a look back and a smile.

Tanner had scooted his chair closer, and his hand warmed her colder one once more. "Do you need anything?"

"I need to call Matt and maybe the social worker to make sure Momma is taken care of while I'm stuck here."

"Done. Your mother's over at Woodcrest. She's doing pretty well. She knows Mrs. Myers and Mr. Hendricks, so she's okay for now."

"Tyler wants to buy the cabin. Or what is left of it."

"I know. Tyler wants to build a place of his own close to the farm and Pap. A man can't live with his grandfather all his life."

Nor could they be under their sister's apron strings. *It's time to let go, Mariah, and move on.*

Lord, this was hard.

She squeezed Tanner's hand. Everything had been taken care of for her. The police had arrested Holt, and Sheriff Brady had assured her as they put her on the gurney for transport that the man would go to prison for a long time.

Her brother Myles was in a rehabilitation center, and Matt oversaw Momma's care.

"There is nothing left for me to do," she whispered.

"How about you focus on getting better so I can take you home. I'd like to see you, Mariah. Every day. If you'll let me?"

"Tanner Evans coming courting over to our farm?" It was something she could hear Momma saying.

"I'm not good at this, Mariah. I have nothing to offer you. Not even a ring, but if you have a little faith in me, I'll get you one. I will take Myles' place at the feed mill part-time until he returns. Tyler and Pete are helping me find side jobs since I've been doing most of the farm work with Pap slowing down and Tyler working."

She brought his hand over her heart. "Tanner," she breathed. "You don't have to buy me a ring."

"I do, Mariah, because I want to slip one on your finger and make you my wife."

She didn't know what to say to that. Mariah fought to

keep her eyes open and not fall asleep. She'd have to ask the doctor to lower the pain medication. A girl needed a clear head to think, especially when she's sort of getting a proposal, and yawning would be rude.

"Are you proposing, cowboy?" It was the term Gail had used. It suited him. More so than 'farm boy.' Tanner Evans had a swagger about him and a smile that could charm any girl.

What once had irritated her ten years ago warmed her veins and made her heart beat a little faster.

Tanner leaned over her, her drooping eyes trying to stay focused on his. She didn't want to wake back up later and find this a dream.

"Will you have me, Mariah? Will you be my wife?" His words were slow and steady like her pulse ticking along with her heart.

She reached up, touching his cheek, drawing him closer— the other hand holding his to her pounding heart. "I'll have you on one condition," she said.

"And which one is that?" he asked.

"That you forgive yourself for what happened. I can see it in your eyes. It wasn't your fault Tanner. Not then and not now."

He tilted his head into her palm. Those golden-boy eyes held hers. *Lord, I love this man;* she thought.

"I made a promise to Mark. While in that car together, he was dying, and I didn't know it. I promised I'd always look after you. I couldn't stop what happened."

"Are you asking me because of a promise?"

"I spent ten years dwelling on what I lost, grieving Mark and the accident. And you." He kissed her palm. "You were Mark's sister. We had a code. He told me to stay away, but even then, he knew before I did. I have thought of you more often than not over the years. Thinking of you helped me get through my time. I love you, Mariah."

"To have and to hold? 'Til death do us part?" she whispered, knowing she was pushing him.

"Just don't get reshot. I have never been more afraid or felt helpless in my life. Watching you rise off your knees, and that guy with a gun to your head easily took off another ten years of my life."

She saw it in the lines forming across his forehead and around his mouth. She wanted to kiss him but knew she couldn't yet. Not until she told him. "I think I can handle that if you can handle dealing with my family."

Matt had only come back around, would her and Tanner's relationship cause another rift?

"Then I'll take that as a yes. Matt gave me his blessing this morning."

"He did?" Her hand almost slipped away from his face.

"You were sleeping. I didn't want to wake you since you've been in and out of it for the past 48 hours. You don't think I'd ask you before I asked your brother?"

"Of course not." She brought him down to her and kissed him. He planted a hand beside her head to keep from crushing her.

His kiss was like the first jolt of caffeine in the morning. Whatever pain medication they'd given her in her IV had no chance of pulling her back into slumber when Tanner's kiss awakened her.

She wrapped her arms around his neck, kissing him back, trying to lift herself off the pillows. Then hissed as a sting of pain in her upper arm and thigh reminded her why she was in this hospital bed.

"It is, yes, isn't it?" He pulled away.

"Yes," she tried to pull him back, his kiss the best medicine in the world.

A throat cleared, and Dr. Harrison stood with a clipboard in his arms.

"We'll have plenty of time for this when you get out of

here," Tanner whispered in her ear. The warmth of his breath sent shivers tingling down her spine at the promise of what was to come.

ABOUT THE AUTHOR

Growing up on a farm in Pennsylvania, Susan Lower yearned for adventure. A woodsy gal, Susan prefers camping over going to the beach any day. Still a farm girl at heart, Susan writes fast action reads filled with cowboys, heroes, and hope. She writes both western historical and contemporary romances, romantic suspense, and has been itching to one day write a mystery or thriller. Christmas is her favorite holiday, and she loves to write resilient characters struggling to overcome the complications of life while holding their values and strengthening their faith.

Made in United States
Cleveland, OH
22 January 2026